# DIWALI IN MUZAFFARNAGAR

**Tanuj Solanki**'s first novel, *Neon Noon*, received critical acclaim post its release in 2016, and was shortlisted for the Tata Literature Live! First Book Award. His short fiction has been published in the *Caravan*, *Hindu Business Line*, *DNA*, *Out of Print*, and several other publications. He lives in Mumbai with his wife.

To,
Whoever finds this gift.

I hope you enjoy reading it, and if you do, please do consider leaving a review/rating on Goodreads on Amazon. And then, send it out into the world for the next book lover to discover it!

Thank you
:)

April 25, 2018

## Advance Praise for *Diwali in Muzaffarnagar*

Intimacy and inevitable grief collide often in these haunting stories of kinship and frayed ties. Solanki writes with great sensitivity about women and men who circle around their roles in families and society, seeking identities that free them from the past, even as its hold on them remains insoluble. These are stories that ache with love, and brave the knowledge that only rarely does love transcend its attendant pain.

– Sharanya Manivannan

Solanki not only surprises me with his craft and voice but also revives my interest in short stories. His observations are precise, his language lyrical and his style extremely pleasing. *Diwali in Muzaffarnagar* is not just another collection of well-written stories. It is a reminder that we have a goldmine of tales from which gifted writers like Solanki can bring us dazzling pieces.

– Anees Salim

Solanki gradually opens a door into a fascinating world, putting to the sword patronizing myths about small-town India.

– Prayaag Akbar

Solanki's stories are brilliantly nuanced, that quintessential mofussil north Indian town – Muzaffarnagar, in this case – reflected in them with all its intimacy and prejudices. The small town is never romanticized, though, and there is an admirable matter-of-fact quality to how the stories progress and end.

– Hansda Sowvendra Shekhar

# DIWALI IN MUZAFFARNAGAR

TANUJ SOLANKI

HarperCollins *Publishers* India

Published in India in 2018 by HarperCollins *Publishers*
A-75, Sector 57, Noida, Uttar Pradesh 201301, India
www.harpercollins.co.in

2 4 6 8 10 9 7 5 3 1



P-ISBN: 978-93-5277-593-4
E-ISBN: 978-93-5277-594-1



Typeset in 11/14 Adobe Caslon Pro
by Jojy Philip, New Delhi 110 015

Printed and bound at
Thomson Press (India) Ltd

*To my father*

# *Contents*

# *The Sad Unknowability of Dilip Singh*

The never-to-be-famous writer Dilip Singh died of his own hand in the winter of 2006. He was twenty-nine. His mother returned from her grocery rounds on the unfortunate day of his death and found him hanging from the ceiling fan, one of her plain widow's saris wrapped tightly around his strained neck. In the hope that her son still had some life in him, she drew a chair (the same chair that Dilip had toppled some time back) beneath his feet and mounted another to untie the noose. Failing to do that, she noticed the loosened plaster around the hook that held the ceiling fan and, in her panic, began to pull the body downward. Some plaster and cement fell on her face, but the body could not be set free. It never occurred to her that had she managed to free it, the heavy ceiling fan, which was from an era when a lot of iron went into those things, would have crushed them both anyway.

Dilip's choice wasn't something that the circumstances, or my understanding of them, added up to. To say that he was a writer is not to say much, for the label is a problematic one. By the time of his suicide, Dilip had written a lot in both English and Hindi, although none of it was published.

He had started writing when he was twenty-three. His

initial outpourings were in the form of poems, and the only people who ever read or heard those were his close friends, who did so only reluctantly, for the verses spoke of a coming apocalypse or a love long lost or the inescapable misery of life, and Dilip's friends, all as young as him, could not find in them anything to connect with. The more sensitive ones among them liked to point out that Dilip's poems were dishonest, for he had himself never experienced anything traumatic, and so when he talked of 'grey skies that gave out a grey piss', or of 'love's half-life', or of 'a beggar's prayers for no rains that season', he sounded phony. I was a friend of Dilip's, probably closer to him than the others, and I too had similar feelings about his early poetry. In our private conversations, I would ask him where he was getting his ideas from. His answers were never satisfactory. He would say that a poet's primary condition is to be ever-sentient of death, or that a poet who doesn't know love's loss is not a true poet, or that misery is the automobile that rams us into the wall of death, et cetera. With hindsight, I have come to understand that phase as one where he was struggling to find his feet in the quagmire that is literature. I also suspect that all of it was under the agony of a broken love affair that none of his friends had been aware of.

But Dilip and his work changed. Between 2001 and 2004, he was excited about writing prose poems, of the sort where a collection of seemingly disparate paragraphs hint at an elusive core (these might be his words), and although he continued to write of death and misery and betrayals, his work now exuded a sense of privacy too. The prose poems registered in one's heart as having been written by a suffering individual. They had in them the scratches of defeat – a defeat not felt or read or imagined, but one experienced in the real. Perhaps this is a mere effect that he created by simply turning to a first-person voice that was more nuanced than his earlier voices. For example, 'the grey sky gave out a grey piss' now went like this: 'After it rained, I walked on the road, looking down, but the vision didn't change even if I looked up to the sky. Everything was the colour of my mind.'

The reasons for this apparent melancholy still escaped me. I tried to talk about it, which was easier now as Dilip was far less obnoxious than he had been earlier. We often sat on the sea front at Marine Drive, where he would read his latest work to me. Even though the subject of his writing was almost always too serious, I assumed he was happy, for he did give off a certain confidence that stemmed from the improvement in his writing. Conversely, he told me that the grim nature of what he wrote about surprised him as well, and might just be a by-product of the grave voices of the writers he was reading in those days. I remember how this statement had relaxed me, and also how honest it had seemed to me, simply because it had in it the hints of a confession. In effect, Dilip was copying the writers he admired, but at least he had the courage to accept that. Whether his work of that time could be called original or not, I do not know, although I do feel sad that no one will ever be able to give an authoritative answer. The little that I have quoted is from what I have retained over the years.

And then, as if out of a perverse logic, Dilip was struck by real pain: his father died of a massive heart failure. I and other friends went to his house to express our condolences. There I saw Dilip, standing in a corner of the living room where he would eventually end his life. He looked stunned rather than distraught. He did not utter a single word to any of us, and so we all considered it better to leave and allow the family to grieve for their loss.

Two weeks later, I received a phone call from him. He sounded excited, which confused me. He told me that he had written a long prose poem, which a magazine of national circulation had decided to publish in its upcoming issue. I did not miss the impropriety of such a reaction only two weeks after losing a father; nevertheless, I congratulated Dilip wholeheartedly. He wanted to meet me at Marine Drive the next day, so that he could read this poem to me. I agreed.

The poem was about a ten-year-old boy who had a world of his own – a lush, strange world full of esoteric notions. The poem was difficult to understand, not merely because of the complexities of its language. Then there came a revelatory passage, in which the child watches his father hit his mother with a rod, and then a sequence where the mother shows the mark of that violence to the child. The details of the mother baring her thigh to the child to show him the mark were unnerving. I realized then that this was a personal experience, although the end, where the child buries the rod under a peach tree, might have been fabricated.

After Dilip was done reading, I was hesitant to provide any reaction at all. But then I told him that what he had written seemed to me like something that had happened to him. Dilip grew silent and stared at the horizon for what seemed a long time. When we resumed talking, it was about an entirely different topic, and then we got up and went to a nearby café to have some cold coffee. The poem was deliberately forgotten. Although I remember how, in the taxi ride back home that day, I had thought of it as a veritable masterpiece.

Dilip called me a couple of days later. It was quite late in the night, and I could only hear an incoherent blabbering from the other side. It was as if he was heavily intoxicated, which was strange because I knew that Dilip never drank. I could think of nothing better than to cut the call and reach out to him later. Next morning, when I visited his house on my way to work, his mother told me that he had left the previous night. He has gone to the Himalayas for some time, she said, and added something about how disturbed he had been since his father's demise. I was confused, but then I shrugged and got on with my life. What else could I do?

I did, of course, retain some interest in my friend, and so the next month I got a copy of the magazine in which his work should have been published. It was not there! My confusion regarding him was now mixed with guilt, for I thought that maybe he chose not to publish the poem because I had found it to be too personal. I rang his house, but his mother told me that he had still not returned. She had no contact number or address to locate him, and had no clue about the poem due to be published in the magazine. For a while I wondered if Dilip had lied to me about being accepted for publication. But why would he do that? To make me listen to his poem with respect, with approval? It made me ask questions of myself: had I thought of the poem as a masterpiece because it was due for publication? This would mean that Dilip had conned me, and that I had conned myself too. Now I wasn't even sure if his father had really hit his mother with an iron rod. And if that wasn't true, was the poem then a masterpiece because it had appeared so real and personal?

It was six more months before Dilip finally returned to Bombay – with a large beard and webby eyes. He had decided to be jobless; apparently, his father had left behind a considerable amount in insurance money. We got into the habit of meeting at Marine Drive every Saturday evening, where he would read some of his writings to me. I kept my distance emotionally and never broached the topic of the unpublished poem. He was writing short stories now – stories that seldom had more than two characters who met each other for the first and the last time in them. He either never sought publication or was never accepted by anyone. I felt that he didn't have anything substantial to write about, and was therefore writing about the transitory nature of human encounters – how we grow intimate with strangers and then part without much ado. While this template persisted in general, the settings and the tones and the timelines changed dramatically from story to story, and the intensity of the connection that the two characters felt for each other also varied substantially. Sometimes there would be a third party or an object or an idea that was important to both the characters. As weeks passed, as those weeks became months, September-October-November, as life settled into a routine for me and probably for Dilip too, I began to enjoy these weekly rendezvous and came to be excited about knowing the identities of the two strangers that my friend would set in a story next.

And then that Friday morning in late December, I was at work, probably toiling over a presentation or a spreadsheet. There was a tiny suicide note, in which he blamed himself and nobody else. In the days to follow, I took it upon myself to comfort his mother as much as I could. I would visit her every other day. It was in one of these meetings that she narrated her struggle with her son's lifeless body. She eventually came to tell me that Dilip had burnt all his writings before hanging himself. She had noticed flakes of ash drifting on the living room floor before she had looked up to find her son. Then she cried, and then I cried, and the crying went on till it exhausted itself, at which point the silence became so oppressive that I ran out of the house.

## *My Friend Daanish*

Four months after my sixteenth birthday, Papa bought me a Honda Activa. I didn't know anything about it till the moment he drove it in and parked it in our front yard. For the first few minutes, I believed that he had bought the scooter for himself, and that was happiness enough, for I imagined that I would get to use it every once a while. Then he called me closer and demo-ed the electric-start mechanism. The scooter settled into a low hum. Meanwhile, Mummy had started the process of finger-painting an orange swastika just above the headlight. She smiled at Papa once, and since a smile was something rare between them, I knew immediately that the moment was special. Then the two of them looked at me and laughed together, and I understood that the Activa was for me.

The swastika would be an eyesore, I knew, but I didn't tell Mummy that because, in my assessment, it was she who had made the scooter possible in the first place. Many times over the previous year, she had beleaguered papa with descriptions of how I *ploughed* the whole town with my bicycle, how I huffed from school to the first tuition class, then on to the second, and then on to the third, how I came home exhausted around 9 p.m. and then failed to put much muscle into my Physics Chemistry Maths. Papa had resisted Mummy's exhortations by citing how, in his own time, he had had to hang onto the rear ends of buses to reach his school every day, how there had been no tuitions then, how teachers never turned up, and so on. But then I topped eleventh standard and things changed.

My results had stoked my parents' dreams of an IIT selection, and the scooter was less a reward and more an investment for the all-important twelfth standard. That it was not the PCM marks that had pushed me to the top spot but a ten-point cushion I had over everyone else in English was not known to them. (Only Bharat Goel had scored more marks than me in English, but he had scored miserably in other subjects, and was anyway better known as the only one who had contributed poems – all signed pretentiously as 'B' – to the annual school magazine.) Another thing was that topping the class was not that difficult after tenth, since there wasn't any relevant competition left. It was common practice among the brighter students in Muzaffarnagar to leave the town for Kota, Meerut or Delhi, where better coaching for competitive exams was available.

Not everyone grazed the right grass, however, and there were some bad stories, too. Like of Shivang Gupta, once the Holy Angels' Convent School topper, who had gone to Kota to ace engineering, but had ended up failing the board exams. Rumour was that he had started drinking alcohol and had even begun chewing gutkha. A girl named Khyati Sharma, who had shifted to Delhi after tenth, had eloped with a criminal-type boy. Such stories, of which there was at least one each year, might have had some impact on my parents. 'You will be with us in Muzaffarnagar, safe and healthy,' Mummy had said on the question of leaving the city. 'You'll just have to develop the habit of self-study,' Papa had added.

As for me, I didn't mind staying one bit. At that time, I didn't have any concept of living away from parents, and I was happy I would be home for two more years.

Once Mummy was done with her rituals, Papa and I went for a ride. I drove the scooter in the tiny lanes of Jat Colony. The drive was incident-free, except for the one time when a cow's tail brushed against the headlight. This happened because some of the houses in the colony had mini-cowsheds built right on the road, and manoeuvring the scooter sometimes required going rather close to a tethered cow's rear.

Satisfied with my driving on the tiny lanes, Papa asked me to turn towards Mahavir Chowk. 'Let's see if you can deal with traffic,' he said. I drove around the circle and took one of the roads branching off it – the one going towards Sadar Bazaar. After ten minutes or so, Papa got bored and said, 'Six years of cycling have trained you well. You can ride the scooter decently enough, I think.'

'It won't be a problem,' I agreed.

We didn't talk after that for some time. It was when I was parking the scooter in our front yard that Papa said, 'Just don't do anything stupid with it.'

'Like riding over bumpy places? Potholed roads? Over sand?' I asked, just to be funny.

'You know what I mean,' Papa grunted.

I guess I knew what Papa meant. Muzaffarnagar was a peaceful town, except when it bared its ugly side. And the exceptions were many. The town had a particularly direct way of dealing with any trouble between teenaged boys and girls. Four years back, when an excited eleventh standard guy had pinched a girl's bottom outside a tuition class, the violent mayhem that ensued had ultimately led to the imposition of an unsaid rule: separate tuition timings for boys and girls. Rarely did tuition teachers take the risk of calling boys and girls together; if and when that was done, they ensured the two groups sat at a token distance from each other.

A mandatory change for me after Class X had been the change of school. Till tenth, I had been in Holy Angels' Convent School, an institution run primarily by middle-aged Malayali sisters affiliated to some big Christian mission (I don't remember which). Although the sisters allowed boys and girls to mingle without question, the prospect of continued mingling after a certain age was identified by them as an administrative – and even mission-threatening – challenge, which was why the school turned girls-only after tenth. The boys were asked to leave, which wasn't a great thing for us, because Holy Angels' was considered the best in the district, and one that gave good competition to the English-medium schools in the neighbouring districts of Meerut and Haridwar. Boys who didn't move out of the town had to shift to Sanatan Dharm (S.D.) Public School, which was the best option if one wanted to stay English-medium. The shift meant that our girl friends in Holy Angels', whom we had grown up with since kindergarten, were left behind. Long friendships were broken, as were some fledgling romances. In fact, the last month in Holy Angels' would turn out to be quite dramatic for every passing batch. Some of the girls, it was rumoured, bestowed kisses upon their boyfriends in the shed behind the basketball court. I remember that Gunjan, the prettiest girl of our batch, had received a lot of proposals (proposals for what, I wondered) from my friends around that time.

At any rate, the shifting of schools made us boys and girls aware of being boys and girls. That it happened around the time when our own bodies were intent on establishing that difference made it more difficult.

For migrants from Holy Angels', things were difficult in S.D. Public. We were all crammed together in a single section, and since there were no girls around us anymore, we didn't really know how to *be* with each other. Friendships were shaken even among us, as it slowly became apparent that a lot of our equations with each other were in fact mediated by the girls. My friendship with Apoorv, Ankush, and Tarun, all of whom had been great friends, altered. It was in this new environment that I came closer to Daanish, with whom my relationship had only been cordial in the years at Holy Angels'. It won't be wrong to say that I had mostly watched him from a distance then.

Daanish had a cool carelessness about the studies business – something that I admired. He was cool in other little things as well – in how he took haphazard notes for all subjects in a single notebook; how he played with his ball pen, making it rotate endlessly on his thumb; how he ran his fingers through his hair every now and then; how he played with his cell phone inside the class (this was a time when only two or three students in the entire class had a cell phone; I didn't). He was extremely handsome when the rest of us had at best been cute, and some of my girl friends in Holy Angels' used to call him *Dadonis*. Gunjan was no doubt attracted to him, and must have been disappointed when it turned out that Daanish wasn't part of the crowd that had its heart set on her. He always put on a lot of deodorant, and it was because of him that I started using deodorant in Class XI myself, after convincing my parents that the cycling was making me sweat a lot and that other students complained about my body odour. Of course, the use of deodorants continued even after I had acquired the scooter.

In eleventh at S.D., our engineering futures were at stake, and the studies business was heating up day by day. Tuitions were inevitable. Daanish and I went to the same tuition classes. Although he never missed school, his attendance in the tuition classes was erratic. The tuition masters could hardly bother about that. They ran their enterprises in small rooms inside their houses where more than thirty students jostled with each other for seating space; it was better for everyone when someone skipped class.

No one knew where Daanish went when he skipped tuition. Since the beginning of eleventh, he had a Royal Enfield Bullet with him, on which he sat with a regal posture, never slouching like some of the other kids who owned motorbikes and thought slouching on motorbikes was cool. The Bullet, the only one among students in the whole of Muzaffarnagar, looked like a monster when it stood next to the other bikes outside a tuition master's house. Sometimes, when Daanish came late to a tuition class, the loud percussive sound from the street would stop the proceedings and everyone, including the tutor, would wait till he entered the tiny classroom.

When I finally got a scooter in twelfth grade, my friendship with Daanish deepened. Between tuitions, he would ride his bullet next to my Activa, and we would talk about the English Premier League, an interest we shared. It helped that both of us supported Manchester United, and Daanish would often give me updates on the club's performance in the weekly matches, which I could never watch, owing to the awkwardness I imagined would ensue if I asked my parents for permission. I guess Daanish liked talking to me too, for his attendance in tuitions improved after I got my scooter. That I had topped eleventh might have been a factor as well.

Daanish wasn't great at studies, but even he knew that he couldn't mess up twelfth standard. He asked for my help every now and then – something I was always happy to provide in school or as we stood next to our vehicles between tuitions. For me, the affinity with Daanish was perhaps because he was someone I couldn't be. There were things he knew and did that I, and other boys like me, who were trained by their families to value studies over everything else, could not. His was a practical awareness and knowledge about the world – something that always caught me off guard, for it made me question why it had been impossible for me to know such things. It was true, for example, that he couldn't explain the concepts behind the diffraction of light, or why the sky appeared blue, that he didn't know how a Polaroid lens really worked, but he knew which lanes to take at what time of the day to avoid the sun's glare. He had a penchant for finding shortcuts, had travelled to Dehradun all alone, had even driven his Bullet to Delhi once. He couldn't explain the process of refining crude oil, but he knew the mileage of all cars and motorbikes. When he said ten kilometres, it was as if he knew how long ten kilometres really were, as if he grasped every metre of those ten kilometres. He couldn't explain how internal combustion engines worked, or the exact difference between petrol and diesel engines, or two- and four-stroke engines, but he knew where to find a spark plug in a motorbike, and was the kind of person who could guess what was wrong with a two-wheeler by the roar of its engine.

I remember how, during the first few months of my Activa's life, he would accompany me to the Honda service station whenever the vehicle needed servicing, and would give very specific instructions to the mechanics, asking them to check this, check that, replace this, tighten that, et cetera. It was all Chinese to me; yet I liked listening to him talk, since I learnt that there were other kinds of valuable knowledge in the world. We would leave my scooter at the service station on those days, and I would ride pillion on his Bullet to the tuitions.

One afternoon, while rushing from the physics tuition to the chemistry one, we got into a conversation about how boring inorganic chemistry really was, and how it was highly improbable that any of those producing-metal-from-ore processes would ever help us in real life. Such 'useless fundae', as he used to call them, irritated Daanish. The only physics chapter he had liked was electrostatics, which had a section on rubbing material A with material B to create a static charge that could be used to give someone a nice little twitch in class.

At one point, Daanish asked me: 'Do you want to bunk today?'

I looked at him in amusement. 'I've never done it. What will we do?' I said.

'Something.'

'What?'

'We can have dosas at Sangam. And some Coca Cola.'

'This is what you do when you don't come to tuitions?'

'Sometimes. Sometimes I do other things.'

'Like what?'

'Like … I just roam around, go for a ride on my bike. Sometimes I go watch a movie at Meenakshi.'

'And what if the teacher calls home and reports our absence?'

'Eh – you think they care? They have never called my house.'

They never called your house because you are Muslim, I wanted to say, but didn't. I agreed to bunk the class.

This brings me to another difference that boys like us became aware of after tenth standard – that of being Hindus and Muslims, and what that entailed.

Apparently, Muslims in Muzaffarnagar, making up roughly half of the population in the town, did not prefer their children joining a school whose name had the words 'sanatan dharm' in it. Sending children to a convent school was okay, for Christianity was a negligible religion in Western U.P. (although the church at Sarwat Gate paid the converts well; we came to know this when our maths teacher in Holy Angels' changed from Kundan to Christopher), but being in S.D. was less acceptable. This was because S.D. Public School was a Hindu school, and although it seldom exceeded Holy Angels' in the frequency of its religious messaging, the way it went about things somehow made them more visible. Morning prayers in Holy Angels' could be in Hindi or English, using hymns and songs that were secular and catholic in turn. Morning prayers in S.D. were almost exclusively in Hindi, despite it being an English-medium school, and were exclusively in praise of Hindu gods. A miniature Jesus hung on a miniature cross in each classroom in Holy Angels': we never noticed it, either because of its size or because we were too acclimated to the classrooms. The Saraswati sculpture in the assembly hall in S.D. was large and impossible to miss, and, unlike the Jesus, greeted a mass of students, a majority of whom had a picture of the same goddess in their houses as well. In Holy Angels', the only rule during prayers was to join our hands; some made a fist of one hand and covered it with other, some joined open palms, some interlaced their fingers. In S.D., almost everyone prayed with joined palms. Boys like me and Daanish, Holy Angels' boys who were a minority in S.D., adjusted to this without ever really being asked to.

No one talked about these things. We had begun to understand them on our own, and to sense that others understood them too. In my growing-up years at Holy Angels', where the distinction between Hindu and Muslim was never much of a big deal, I had quite a few Muslim friends, like Daanish Alam, Mohammad Usman, Kashif Bilal, Syed Ali Akbar, Syed Ali Mehdi and Baqar Abbas. Of these, only Daanish and Usman joined S.D. in eleventh standard. The rest moved out of Muzaffarnagar, and not because of academic reasons. Now that I think of it, academic reasons couldn't have meant much for Muslim students, for none of them was very good at studies. They seemed to have different priorities. Maybe their families had different concerns. Or perhaps my understanding is incorrect.

But then, this is why I thought the tuition masters would never care to call Daanish's parents.

Daanish and I went to Gol Market that day for dosas and Coke at Sangam's. When the cook was making the dosas on the open-air pan, Daanish stood right next to him and gave him instructions. He seemed to know which ingredients would do what. I was impressed that his worldly knowledge extended to cooking as well.

The hour or so that we spent at Sangam left me with a strange feeling, and when dusk fell around us, it felt as if it were the first dusk of my life. I was probably looking at the sky at that time of the day after a gap of a couple of years.

After this initiation, the frequency of my bunking with Daanish climbed steadily. Sometimes Usman and Ankush would join us if it was physics or maths that we were bunking, for they didn't share the chemistry tuition with us. Ankush liked to smoke. The bunks would allow him to smoke a cigarette and then kill the stench for the rest of the hour. We were careful: we never bunked any single subject too much in close succession. We wouldn't even go to restaurants all the time; we could just pass time standing in a little lane, talking about football and cricket, or about the girls we had left behind in Holy Angels'. Sometimes we would see an old classmate going to her tuition, and would give her a knowing nod. The resulting smile on her face would warm our hearts.

Daanish and I became even better friends because of these bunking sessions. On all weekday evenings, after the tuitions or bunks were over, there would come that point, at Meenakshi Chowk on G.T. Road, when Daanish would turn his Bullet right towards the Muslim area of Khalapaar and I would go straight towards Jat Colony. But this happened only after we had had a lengthy pause on the side of the road and planned the adventures of the next day. Our discussions started eating into the time I was supposed to be saving because of the scooter.

One fine Sunday morning – all our tuitions were off on Sundays – Daanish turned up at my house unexpectedly. He unlatched the front gate on his own and knocked on the door that opened to the living room. I was sitting there at that time, but it was my mother who opened the door. He politely refused her invitation to come inside and asked for me, mumbling something about an extra class that the chemistry teacher was intent on taking. She then asked him for his name and, hearing it, turned to look at me with an awkward smile. I should confess that I too felt a bit nervous seeing Daanish turn up like that outside my house. But I was always nervous when any of my friends turned up at home, since I felt the need to hide my friendships from my parents. How did he know where I lived? He must have asked Ankush, or someone else, I reasoned.

Daanish looked well-groomed for that time of the day. I was still in my pyjamas, and the thought that I couldn't match him in looks no matter how hard I tried crossed my mind. I ushered him outside to talk to him on the street, somehow certain that he would refuse to come inside even if I asked him to. Daanish didn't seem to care. He was more eager to reveal his plan to me. He commanded me to tell my mother that it was indeed very important to attend the extra class, to get ready in five minutes, and to be out on my scooter as soon as possible.

'But where will we go?' I asked him.

'We will go to Harmony,' he said, and added a mischievous smile to that.

Harmony was a mall on the Delhi–Dehradun highway, located towards Delhi, some eight to ten kilometres away from Muzaffarnagar. It had everything – McDonald's, Subway, a game parlour called Zone 7, a four-screen multiplex called Cinestar. I had never been there, although I had heard that it was fantastic. Families travelling on the highway preferred to stop there for a break, and I had heard (from Daanish) that there were pretty girls in the restaurants all the time. I had never talked to my parents about going there, for I sensed that it would be prohibited for me. This could be for multiple reasons – the fact that reaching Harmony required crossing Soojdo Choongi, a Muslim-majority village that wasn't deemed *friendly*; the fact that it was on a national highway, which meant greater risk for scooterists; the fact that the restaurants there sold chicken items, which was a problem because non-veg was a strict no in my family; and so on.

'Very well then, let's go,' I said, the excitement making

me whisper. 'But I don't have any money in my wallet. And I cannot ask my mother for money right now. It will make her suspicious.'

'Did I say anything about money?'

So we left my house in five minutes. On the way to Harmony, Daanish's Enfield and my Activa kept pace with each other. I wasn't speeding as much as Daanish was going slow. Every now and then I looked at his long hair blowing in the wind. They were the colour of KitKat, I thought. I wished I could keep long hair like him. When I was a child, my father would ask the barber to do a fauji cut on me. As I looked at Daanish's hair, I wondered if I could let go being a fauji now, now that I was seventeen.

We parked our vehicles in the maze-like parking lot in the basement of Harmony Mall and went straight to McDonald's. In the crowd there, one could see women in burqas, sardar men, men with kufi caps on, girls in shorts, women working – a mix that was impossible to find inside any restaurant in Muzaffarnagar. Everyone seemed to have only one concern there – the eating of burgers and fries. Daanish insisted that I eat a chicken burger. I dithered, but then decided to give it a try: I had already broken a few rules that day.

'It's like paneer, isn't it?' Daanish said as I nervously bit into my burger.

'I'm trying not to smell anything,' I said.

'Chicken has no smell.'

'It does.'

'Don't you like the taste?'

'It's okay.'

'Don't tell your parents.'

'I won't. By the way, you guys make it in your kitchen, right?'

'Of course. My mother cooks amazing butter chicken.'

'My mother would faint at the very idea,' I said.

'I've always wanted to know,' Daanish said.

'What?'

'Aren't we killing something when we are eating vegetables?'

'Meaning?'

'You remember biology? Fruits and vegetables are for plants' reproduction.'

'So?'

'So when you eat a ... um ... cauliflower ... you're probably eating future cauliflower plants, aren't you?'

'So?'

'You are eating future life, man. Vegetarians are doing as much killing as non-vegetarians, no?'

'Bullshit.'

'What bullshit? It's true. I just explained it to you.'

Our conversation tapered off as there were pretty girls in the restaurant to get distracted with. In my head, I shuffled Daanish's logic about vegetarian food. Its simple irrefutability made me smile.

After McDonald's, we went to Zone 7 and alternated between the video games for hours. Daanish paid for everything. We lost track of time. By the time we exited the mall it was late afternoon. I was sure my parents would be curious, even worried. I grew nervous at the prospect of having to make up multiple excuses.

'Just tell them you went for a movie after the tuition,' Daanish told me.

'That won't do,' I said.

'Why can't you tell them the truth?'

'Did you tell your parents the truth?'

'I could.'

On our way back, I wondered what Daanish's folks were like. I didn't know what his father did for a living, but I knew that Daanish had an elder brother who had migrated to Dubai after a hotel management course in Delhi. In my eyes, the money for Daanish's clothes, his Bullet, his hair colour, his deodorant, his cell phone, all came from Dubai, and it sometimes made me jealous that I didn't have an elder brother like he did. I knew, however, that if I had an elder brother, he would not have been allowed to do a hotel management course after studying science. That would just be inconceivable in my family.

That evening, my parents were quieter than usual. It was only at dinner that Mummy spoke.

'He went with someone called Daniyal.'

At first I thought it was okay to let it pass, but then I corrected her. 'Daanish,' I said.

'Daanish, Daniyal, same thing.'

'No, it's two different names,' I replied.

Mummy looked at me as if irritated by my insistence that the right name be used. Then she turned towards Papa. 'Right at the living room door,' she said, complainingly. 'Didn't even knock on the outer gate.'

'Everyone who comes to our house does that,' I retorted.

'Where were you after the tuition?' Papa asked me now.

'We went for a movie.'

'You and Daanish?'

'No, there were others too.'

'Which movie?'

'That … the one about the rings.'

'You've never done anything like this before,' Mummy announced.

I didn't respond to that. There were some moments of

silence, after which my parents began discussing something else.

By January, our pre-board exams had already taken place, and school opened only two days in a week. The tuitions were also closed, except for the mock exams held on Saturdays or Sundays, which the tuition masters conducted without charging any fee. On Daanish's advice, I did not tell my parents that the tuitions were closed and that the fee had been waived. This allowed us to go gallivanting for more than a few hours every day. Moreover, it left me with nine hundred rupees of extra pocket money: it could have been eighteen hundred rupees, but I couldn't lie completely – I told my parents that the tuition masters had all halved their fees. With the excursions, I sometimes doubted my sincerity in preparing for the competitive exams. It was as if I was realizing that I didn't really care about being in a big college. The thought hollowed me out, and to dispel it, I convinced myself that the time spent with Daanish was for the good, as being in the house all the time could also have a negative effect on my temperament for studies. I was confident of getting into a decent college for my B.Tech. But it would just be that – a decent college. My parents' dream of me getting into an IIT was unlikely to be fulfilled. It was rare for a student in Muzaffarnagar to be selected to an IIT. The tuitions were just not good enough, I told myself.

Soon came 14 February, Valentine's Day. In Holy Angels', it had been a special day since Class VII. The girls would bring chocolates to school, and the boys would sneak in flowers. The flowers could be any type – roses were preferred, but difficult to procure, and I remember even marigold being used. I myself never participated in the flowers-and-chocolate business in Holy Angels'. I had seen how the number of flowers brought to school that day was always larger than the number of flowers given to girls. Most guys could just not pick up the courage to hand the flower, and I suspected I would be one of those if I tried.

Daanish, I remember from the V-Days in ninth and tenth, would get multiple roses to the school and would manage to give all of them away. His advances were never taken seriously, for any girl receiving a rose from Daanish knew that there were four others like her. There was much frolic about this – the girls would tease *Dadonis* about his multiple crushes, something he would laugh about.

For this V-Day, Daanish's plan was to take girls out to Harmony – have the bigger burgers at McDonald's, play some video games at Zone 7, watch a movie or something, maybe even try some kissing in the basement. He had included Usman, Ankush and me in his plan. But Usman backed out immediately, saying Daanish was out of his mind. When the time came to decide whom we wanted to go out with, Daanish announced he was going to ask Gunjan. Hearing this, Ankush backed out of the trip as well. Ankush and Gunjan were neighbours, and there was something wrong between them. They had not been on speaking terms for several years now.

I decided I wanted to go out with Anjana. She and I had shared a bench at school till Class VI, after which strict Sister Venetia, who taught history well but completely confused us in civics, made boys and girls sit in different rows. Anjana and I had often joked about being boyfriend–girlfriend when we grew up, and I hoped that she too remembered the days when it was easier for us to say silly things like that – days when childhood was present at either end of our present.

In a meeting at Meenakshi Chowk a couple of days before the big day, Daanish told me that Gunjan had said yes to going out with him. He asked me about Anjana, and I told him that she had refused to go to Harmony. 'I don't blame her,' I added.

'You don't blame her?' Daanish said. 'What does that mean? You blame Ricky Ponting, then?'

'It's a sensible decision,' I said. 'It is risky to take the girls so far out.'

'What risk? It would have been fun,' Daanish replied. 'And you don't get anything in life without risk.' The irritation was clear on his face. Gunjan would also say no to the plan now that it was just the two of them.

Then my patience ran out, and a giggle burst through from me.

'What?' Daanish asked. 'What, you bastard? She said yes?'

'She did say no to Harmony, but she said we could meet somewhere inside the town.' I think I was grinning with jubilation, not least because I had been able to make Daanish depend on me for something.

It took a moment for him to reconcile with the change in plans. But after that he asked excitedly, 'So, any ideas?'

We decided to go to Nandi in the Nai Mandi area. It was not that there were many options. Luckily for us, 14 February fell on a day when Holy Angels' was open, so Gunjan and Anjana didn't have to make any excuses to get out of their homes. We would not have had them bunk school, for that would have meant having to spend a lot of time together, which could have been very problematic, even boring.

So we met the girls after school, outside the large gate of Holy Angels'. Anjana quietly sat behind me on my Activa. I assumed Anjana was shy. I was too excited to worry about it. While on the scooter, I stole glimpses to my right, where the scooter's shadow and our shadows bobbed over the road and the cars and two wheelers and other roadside things; I saw the sunlight between her silhouette and mine, and also how her back was painfully erect, with her arms going behind it to hold the metal frame behind the seat. Her hair was freer, and it somehow delighted me to look at its freedom in the shadow.

Daanish had Gunjan behind him on his bullet, with her hands on his shoulders. When I looked at them, it was with envy – they were the two most beautiful people in Muzaffarnagar.

It took barely five to six minutes to reach Nandi. We parked our vehicles by the road and went inside. Nandi had made a small, restaurant-like area next to the tall displays of food items. We were all excited; nervous laughter emitted from all of us as we sat down after placing our orders at the counter. There was a thrill in doing what we were doing, yes. It felt like breaking some rule, but I wasn't sure which one. Soon, as we bantered, as the roses (sourced by Daanish) and chocolates were given, as sideways hugs were shared with the girls, the other customers at Nandi looked at us as if they had a better idea, as if they understood exactly what we were doing, what rules we were breaking. Their gazes didn't approve of this – of young boys and girls loafing at Nandi and celebrating a day that generally had no business being celebrated in Muzaffarnagar. I looked at

Daanish with concern, which he didn't register. He just winked at me and moved his hand behind Gunjan's chair (she was sitting next to him, obviously). I smiled back but, aware now of the gaze of others, I was sweating.

In the next minute, Anjana touched my hand with her fingers. My hand was below the table, on my thigh. She picked my hand and placed it on her thigh. The sweat on my forehead cooled. I got an immediate and nervous erection. In my mind, the entire clientele at Nandi was looking at that hand of mine, something that was impossible since both Anjana and I were concealed well, sitting behind a table, with our backs to the wall.

Nevertheless, I pulled my hand back. Anjana shifted on her chair. I shifted on mine. I stuffed my mouth with the kachori on the table. She pinched a petal of the rose I had given to her. When I finally looked at her after a minute, she smiled in a forgiving way. That gave me some relief.

After two rounds of snacking, we left Nandi to chit-chat right outside the restaurant, where our vehicles were parked. Gunjan leaned on Daanish's bullet, seeing which Anjana also sat on my Activa. Daanish moved his fingers through his hair. He and Gunjan laughed at something. Anjana slapped me on my shoulder, making a complaint I didn't really register. Will I get married to her, I was thinking. We were perhaps not having fun but only simulating fun. But there was no other way; the excitement was too high. And that's probably why we didn't notice the two men who came up next to our vehicles till they started talking to us.

'What are you doing here, hein?' the larger one among them asked, his hands behind his back.

'What's your problem?' Danish said. He shouldn't have said that, I thought. He was acting tough, showing off.

'Tell us your names. What are your names?' the other one said. He was smoking a cigarette.

'Why?' Daanish replied, standing up and moving towards the two. 'You own this place or what?'

The men moved their gaze towards the girls. 'What are your names?'

The girls told them their names. They weren't sitting on the bikes anymore. I had the weird feeling of being caught in something terrible. Almost in reflex, I moved my keys into the Activa keyhole and unlocked it. The smoking man noticed this.

'So what's your problem, eh?' Daanish said, walking up to the man who had his hands behind his back. They were both the same height, about six feet, the tallest among all present there.

'Tell us your names,' the other man repeated.

'It is Daanish Alam. Now tell me what you intend to do with it.'

'And what's yours?' the men asked me.

'Ankush,' I said. I don't know why I lied.

The man who was smoking stopped a rickshaw that was passing by. 'Girls, you get into this rickshaw and go home.'

'What do you want? Why should they leave?' Daanish tried to intervene.

The girls, terrified, followed the order. Daanish looked at me. He was trying to convey a signal which I couldn't decipher. I was worried because he had talked back to the men and now something bad could happen. The girls glanced back at us from the rickshaw.

'You'll do musalmani here, eh?' the man with the arms behind his back barked, addressing Daanish. I now saw that he was concealing an iron rod behind his back.

'What is that?' I asked the man.

The other man grabbed my throat and said, 'You sure about your name?'

I was stunned – not telling my real name was going to get me beaten. I started mumbling my sorrys.

'That's his name,' Daanish said, and in the next instant, punched the man who held the iron rod.

The man staggered, but did not lose his footing. The other man slapped me, and then pushed me on the Activa. 'Go, or you will also get pulped,' he said. He then punched Daanish on his chest. By now the first man had recovered, and he hit Daanish's shoulder with the rod. Daanish yelped. I started my Activa. The rod had made a swoosh in cleaving the air. And then I heard the swoosh again. This time the rod hit Daanish on the left thigh. I looked at him. He had rage in his eyes, and I knew that he had not registered the pain of the second hit. I saw him lunge at the assaulter and take him to ground. The man poked the rod hard into Daanish's ribs. The other man kicked him in the head. I saw a little burst of blood on the road. My friend was bleeding. There were three more men at the scene now; they had emerged from a neighbouring shop and looked hostile to Daanish.

Daanish was raining punches on the man who had held the rod earlier, but punches and kicks were being delivered to him as well. I manoeuvred the scooter, almost circling the area where the fight was taking place. All I was thinking of was getting out of there. I rolled the accelerator. I did not look back at anything. Looking back did not even occur to me. But after there was a good distance between me and the scene, once I was safe, my vision constricted and my hands started shaking. I had to stop the scooter. I didn't have any coherent thought for the next couple of minutes. In my mind, it was as if a pencil was making too many random criss-crosses, making everything unintelligible.

Then I realized that those goons had assumed that I was Muslim – that's what they meant about me being unsure of my name. Had Daanish saved me then? I heard the sound of an Enfield Bullet, but it was only in my head. My friend Daanish, I thought. 'My friend Daanish,' I mumbled. Daanish was probably still there, fighting. Or having fought. I had a vision of him getting *pulped*, and it sent a cold shudder down my spine. My teeth started chattering. I sat down on the edge of the road. There were people on that road, but none seemed to notice me. Or maybe not much that was wrong with me was visible. I tried to speak out my friend's name, as if uttering his name would change things. But the 'Daanish … Daanish …' that came out of my mouth was worse than a whimper. Save him, a voice inside me said. I shook my head. I realized I was choking, and forced myself to take deep breaths. Nothing bad is going to happen, I told myself. Nothing too bad is going to happen.

I spent five minutes like this, maybe ten, till a man wearing a chequered shirt over loose trousers, around my father's age, came up to me. 'What happened?' he asked. 'Nothing,' I replied, rising to my feet and slapping the dust off my jeans. 'Is this your scooter?' 'Yes.' 'Why are you sitting here like this?' When I couldn't answer, he said, 'Go home, beta. This is your age to study, not to sit on the road.' My age to study, not sit on the road – that was right. I mounted my scooter and started it. I thought of going back to Nandi and checking what had happened to Daanish, but didn't have the courage to do that. The scooter began homewards, running on a decree of its own, but as it did that, I allowed myself to think that Daanish had probably escaped without being too hurt. I cultivated this idea for the immediate comfort that it allowed me. But this lightness was a mistake, something that I would pay for later with a damning weight on my chest.

At that time, however, I had made reaching home my only objective. When the scooter was at Meenakshi Chowk, I tried hard not to look at the point where Daanish and I would usually stand to make or break our numerous plans. There was that Khalapaar road to my right – the road beyond which Daanish's safety lay today. Why did he have to pick a fight, I thought. But would it have mattered? Daanish was like this: bold, brash, and a show-off. Perhaps to distract myself, my mind recalled an incident with the S.D. physics teacher, who was used to beating up the boys on a whim. Once he had punched Daanish on his chest for not bringing the physics textbook to class. The punch had taken the wind out of Daanish's lungs, and for a second he had collapsed on the bench. But then he had risen and looked into his abuser's eyes with such rage that he had had to back off. It was the same fiery look that Daanish had given today to the man with the rod.

After a while, the Company Gardens appeared to my left and the breeze turned nippier. I had to take the first left turn after the garden ended. As I neared home and the distance between the incident and me increased, my ability to lull myself into thinking that nothing too bad would happen also increased. But it was mostly because I was distracting myself, not letting myself think too much about the incident.

The huge Numaish Camp ground, where I had played a lot of cricket before tenth standard, appeared to my right. Muslim kids from Khalapaar used to come to the ground too, but the kids from Jat Colony never played with them. The Muslim kids bowled faster, and we often compared them to the tearaway Pakistani bowlers of the nineties. The dilapidated walls of the Metro Motel passed me by to my left. It was a government-made motel that had been closed for years. But then whose undergarments were drying on the first floor? 'It was never supposed to work,' Papa had said of it, hinting at a government gaffe I had no care for. *My friend Daanish*, I thought. Then I crossed an empty ground to my left, whose only purpose was to house the circus during the annual numaish. I had never been to the circus. *My friend Daanish.* The air above the road I was on would remain misty right till the end of February. At the road's end, I would take a left turn. The third house to the right would be mine.

*My friend Daanish.*

I opened the gate and parked the scooter in the front yard. Then I went inside the living room, where Mummy was turning the pages of the knitting issue of a Hindi magazine. 'How was the test?' she asked me.

I didn't answer. Then she said, 'Oh but it was an extra class, right? Not a test.'

I walked into my room to change. Then I lay down on my bed and closed my eyes. The events outside Nandi played in my mind vaguely, with some of the actions blurring out. The worry, and the effort I had put in to distract myself, quickly exhausted me. I fell asleep, and was woken up by Mummy after a few hours.

During dinner, Papa asked me a lot of questions about my studies. He wanted to know what I thought the outcome would be, now that the board exams and the competitive exams were close. I guess I looked sick then, for he advised

Mummy to take special care of me. He joked about me being a cricket player getting ready for a big test series.

At one point, he spoke about some tension in the city after a violent incident in the Nai Mandi area. 'Some Muslim kids were creating a ruckus and got a couple of slaps,' he said, 'and the whole of Khalapaar was shouting slogans at Meenakshi Chowk.' I buried my face in my plate, knowing that it would be impossible to protest against his version of the events without revealing that I was present there.

That night, I sat down to practise some maths problems from the chapter on probability. Probability was my weakest area, and it didn't help that I could not really concentrate, for every other problem reminded me of the events of the day.

*The probability of a man hitting a target is 1/4. He tries 5 times. The probability that the target will be hit at least 3 times is ________.*

*Four boys and four girls sit in a row at random. The probability that boys and girls sit alternately is ________.*

And so on.

Next day, the local Hindi bulletin ran a story on Daanish's beating. The first thing I noticed in the story was Daanish's reported age – eighteen years. I was due to turn seventeen in a month's time. It surprised me that in our conversations we had never discovered that he was elder to me. I established a silly connection between Daanish's dexterity and his age, as if all my clumsiness could be explained away by the fact of me being a year younger. Could my cowardice be explained by that, too?

The news story reported that Daanish *and his friends* were celebrating Valentine's Day with *Hindu girls*. I was the only friend there, but the paper seemed to be suggesting that there were more than one. I was relieved by this absence of specifics about anyone other than Daanish. I didn't want to be discovered.

The hospital where Daanish was receiving care, Nisar Hospital, was in Khalapaar. His condition was reported as *stable but not out of harm*. It puzzled me to read that – what was the possible harm? Could he die?

The story also covered the protest by Muslim leaders at Meenakshi Chowk. It then gave space to a statement – which mentioned a 'Salman Khan–Shahrukh Khan culture', something that young boys from Khalapaar wanted to bring to Muzaffarnagar – it was by the spokesperson of a Hindu organization.

The report ended with the city DSP vowing to bring the perpetrators to justice.

It was not I who had discovered the news in the paper. It was Papa, who showed it to me when I was brushing my teeth that morning, the index finger of his right hand pointing at the news. He asked me if the Daanish of the news story was my friend Daanish. I rinsed my mouth and read the news item. I could not feign indifference, but I had no response to his question, so I moved into my room with the newspaper still in my hands. I, in fact, wanted this question, this news, this entire situation to dissolve, to somehow not exist. Papa followed me into the room. He waited for me to read the news, then took the newspaper from me and walked away – all of it without uttering a word. I knew then that there were seeds of some sort of suspicion in him.

In the evening, I found the newspaper on the living room table. I cut out the news item and kept it inside my organic chemistry textbook. I read it again and again, as if it could provide some clue regarding Daanish's well-being.

The next day, my involvement in the incident became clear to my parents. Anjana's father called mine and asked him to *discipline* me. I don't know what else was shared between them.

My confrontation with my parents was not very dramatic. As a child, I'd been hit only occasionally, that too only by my mother. For some time now, I'd not even given my parents a chance to scold me. I hadn't been a bad child, or even an unruly teenager. So I guess they were at a loss to find a way to be cross with me.

We were in the living room, all seated on different sofas. A tense silence reigned till Mummy began: 'I knew from the beginning that that Daniyal was a bad influence.'

I suspected that Mummy had deliberately used the wrong name this time. 'Daanish,' I corrected her again. There was a silence following this correction, this utterance of the right name. She looked at Papa, who looked down towards the floor, as if it was a mistake made by him. There was a rigid expression on his face that I had never seen before, and in those mute seconds I realized that it was disappointment, disappointment with me and probably also with Mummy, or with the tiny world around him; his expression conveyed an intensity that I had never before seen on that face. I got up from the sofa and went to my room, to study.

That night, at around eleven, Papa entered my room and lay down on the bed. I was sitting at my study desk, with my back towards him. I heard the clink of ice on glass from behind me. He was drinking.

'Are you able to study?' he asked me. His slow speech told me that he had already had a couple.

'Yes,' I responded immediately.

He didn't ask another question, and I felt him take a swig

of his drink. In the minute that followed, I somehow gained the courage to speak the truth. 'Actually, no,' I said.

'Hmm?'

'I'm finding it difficult to study.'

'You are worried about your friend?'

'Yes.'

'It could have been you.'

'It couldn't have been me, Papa,' I said, turning towards him. It was a truth that I realized only as I spoke it.

He didn't bother to respond to that. He shifted his posture and took a sip of his whiskey. He looked straight ahead, at the wall before him. I looked down to the floor, getting lost in the patternless granite.

'You have deviated from your path,' he said.

It hurt me to hear that. My gaze fastened on the floor. I did feel guilty for not fighting with my friend in Nai Mandi. But did I have to feel guilty just for being there? Was being there a deviation? Was my friendship with Daanish itself a wrong thing?

'Your tuitions have been off for more than a month,' Papa said then. 'You lied to us.'

A heat rose up from my chest and suffused my face and my ears. I couldn't continue facing him; so I turned my chair towards my desk and starting peering into my books. Behind my back, Papa burped and shifted his position again. I heard a sniffle. I feared that he was crying. It made my throat tighten.

'Saransh beta,' he addressed me, his baritone creaking. 'There was a time … when you were a kid … there was a time when my salary was four thousand rupees and Holy Angels' fees was twelve hundred rupees. You were the only kid in our neighbourhood to study there.'

I buried my eyes in the text on the book, but the formulas

became blurry. Then, fat tears fell on the page. Papa didn't comfort me. After five minutes, when I turned to look at him, I found him asleep with his mouth open and a wetness around his eyes.

From the next day, Papa started using the Activa for his tasks and errands. When Saturday came, he offered to drop me to the tuitions. 'I don't need to go any more,' I told him, 'they're only taking tests.' He nodded slowly, as if taking it in. 'It's better to practise at home,' I added to convince him.

The board exams were approaching. Mummy had Papa buy a heater and placed it in my room. But when they realized that the warmth made me sleepy, the heater was promptly removed. Mummy was nicer to me than usual, and cooked my favourite dishes. On Papa's side, the frequency with which he came into my room at night increased, though he never again carried a drink with him. Often, he came with a Hindi book in his hand, and made every effort – including making late-night tea for both of us – to stay awake as long as possible. This was to make sure that I too stayed awake and studied till at least an hour after midnight.

During this period, I was never explicitly barred from venturing out of the house, but I accepted what was effectively a curfew without any rebellion. My mind, however, wandered towards Daanish and his well-being every now and then. As the day of the first board exam came closer, I grew positive that I would see him there. I would say sorry to him then, and if he hated me for running away, I would accept that hate – this was my resolve.

Two days before the first board exam, Mummy asked

me to go to the nearby shop to buy some curd. I rode on my bicycle, taking in the crisp, late-February air. The short cycle ride took me back a few months, and I even allowed the thought that, all things considered, the scooter had not been a great thing for me.

Then came the day of the first exam. It was maths. Papa used my scooter to drop me to M.G. Public School, which was the exam centre for the students of S.D. Public School. Before the exam began, the students were made to assemble in the lawns in front of the main building. I looked around for Daanish but couldn't find him. I saw Anjana and said 'Hi' to her, but she receded from me as if I were someone who would bring bad luck. I went up to Gunjan then.

'Daanish isn't here,' she said, without looking at me. Her eyes were scanning the area for him.

'I'm sorry,' I said.

'You are sorry? For what?'

'I ran away. I didn't help him.'

Gunjan looked at me with concern. 'What happened to Daanish?' she asked. Before I could attempt an answer, a bell rang and we were ushered in for the exam.

For the next three hours, I struggled with nothing except a four-mark probability problem. The right approach to attack it just wouldn't come to me and, as I grappled with it for more than ten minutes, my mind flashed the Nai Mandi incident a couple of times. Finally, I manoeuvred to get at an answer, but I sensed (with some irony) that there was more than half a chance that I was wrong. As the exam ended and we all spilled out into the lawns, the right solution dawned on me in a flash, leaving a bitter taste in my mouth. I had got 100/100 in maths in the pre-boards; it would only be 96/100 in the main exam now. Then, applying a perverse logic, I accepted this four-mark loss as part of the penance I had to pay for betraying Daanish.

In the lawns, I didn't get a chance to talk to Gunjan again. So I went to the gate, where Papa was waiting. 'How did it go?' he asked me. 'Perfect,' I answered.

Later at home, the exam and the probability problem receded from my thoughts, and I began to worry about Daanish. I could imagine no reason for anyone being absent from a board exam other than that they were completely incapacitated. It had been almost two weeks since the incident, and if Daanish had not recovered from his injuries, it only meant that he had been gravely harmed.

There was a week between the maths exam and the next one, English. Day after day, my worries about Daanish accreted. I feared that he was dead. And what I feared even more was the possibility that I might never come to know of his fate. There was a chance that further news about him had been published in the local newspaper. Papa was the only one who read it in our house, and if there had been any news about Daanish, I knew that he would hide it from me. It wasn't possible for me to go through the pile and look for the news myself: I was never alone in the house.

Two days before the English exam, my anxiety about what had happened to Daanish was at its peak. Fortunately, Papa was not in the house that day, and so when Mummy asked me if I could go and buy some curd, my desperation made me hatch a quick plan to find out about Daanish. Taking the scooter would make Mummy suspicious; so I told her that I wanted to exercise my legs a bit and would take the cycle through a longer route. She agreed reluctantly. Once on my way, I rushed through Jat Colony and reached Mahavir Chowk, from where I took a turn towards Meenakshi Chowk.

I was pedalling the hardest I could. From Meenakshi Chowk, I went straight into Khalapaar. By then, I had been at top speed for ten minutes and my breath needed catching up. So I slowed the cycle down.

Hundred metres into Khalapaar, a mosque appeared to my left. I'd only ever seen this mosque's light-green minarets from one side of Meenakshi Chowk, where Daanish and I would stand after the tuitions. Up close, the structure was unremarkable, but I wondered if it was the one that Daanish's family had been going to with their fervent prayers.

On either side of the mosque were workshops where Muslim men welded big iron strips. The road turned to the left and, at the turn, I saw a meat shop. Just outside it were live chicken inside cuboidal cages. The shopfront had a poster of Shahrukh Khan – probably from a scene in a film that I knew to be at least four–five years old. The whole place seemed, in fact, different from the kind of shops and markets from where we bought our curd, milk, soaps, et cetera.

The road narrowed ahead of me and turned right, with a little lane branching off the left. As I passed that lane, I saw four burqa-clad figures – the smallest among them a child of not more than ten years – inside. It was not as if I had seen such a sight for the first time – Muslim women were not an uncommon sight in the markets of Muzaffarnagar – but I nevertheless felt queer. Was it the added context of Khalapaar? Was it the simple fact of looking at the women (or girls) inside their domain, as one who had come from outside?

As I moved on, I realized that my heartbeat was picking up. I was feeling vulnerable, fearing that at any moment someone could accost me and demand to know my identity – the way it had happened with Daanish in Nai

Mandi. My conspicuousness on that road, in that milieu, might have been my own construction, but its mild terror was undeniable. It was as if I was moving about in a disguise that could slither off any moment. There was something at once common, exceptional and inexplicable about this. And I wondered – just as I was blinking with trepidation at the Urdu lettering on shop boards, or at the crescent-moon finials on small domes, or at the bearded men going about their business – did Daanish too find the swastika, which was a common sight in Jat Colony, or the om sign, or the red thread wound around people's wrists, discomfiting? Why had we never talked about this?

Nisar Hospital was a simple three-storey structure, looking less like a hospital and more like a cheap lodge. From the road, one could see the common balconies to which the patient rooms opened, their railings nearly covered with all the clothes that had been left there to dry. I entered through the broad entrance and found myself in a large room, which had about thirty people waiting. It wasn't difficult to make out that everyone there was a Muslim.

I walked to the reception in the middle of the room. 'I want to make an enquiry about a patient who was admitted here,' I said to the man at the desk.

He directed me to another person sitting at the far end of the reception area. 'Yes?' the man there asked me.

'I want to know about a patient. Whether he's been discharged? What's his health like?'

'What is the name of the patient?' the man asked me. He was probably in his early thirties, had a Muslim beard, and seemed to be wearing kajal in his eyes. There were tobacco stains on his teeth.

'Daanish Alam. He was admitted on the evening of February 14th.'

The man eyed me, and he saw a nervous teenager, sweaty, clean-shaven, a bit red in the ears. Then he checked a fat register. 'Yes, Daanish Alam,' he said, still looking at the register.

'Yes.'

'Who are you?'

'I'm a friend of his.'

'Your name?'

I had the inexplicable urge to say Ankush again. I resisted it. 'Saransh Malik,' I said.

The man looked up from the register, paused, then looked down again.

'We are … we were … school friends.'

'He was badly hurt. Broken right arm, broken ribs,' the man said. 'And … head injury.'

'So, what's happened to him?'

'He was referred to Meerut on the 19th of February.'

This only meant that the injuries were severe. People were referred to Meerut only when the Muzaffarnagar doctors couldn't help them.

'Do you know how he is? Is there any way I can know?' I asked the man. I could hear my own voice quavering.

'Were you with him when it happened?'

I couldn't answer in yes or no. I had an absurd vision of Daanish being insensate and receiving electric shocks. Tears welled up in my eyes.

'He must be alive,' the man said, almost in sympathy. 'If he was dead, someone would have told you.'

I wiped my tears, thanked the man, and walked out of the hospital. I sat on my bicycle. In the journey out of Khalapaar, I didn't notice its peculiarities so much. My friend Daanish, that's all I could think.

Back home, I found Mummy in a fit of rage. I had taken an hour and a half for something that never took more than ten minutes. It didn't help that I had forgotten to buy the curd. To her inquiries about where I had been, I responded by hiding my face so firmly in my palms that no amount of her strength could make me show it.

Although I couldn't make it to the IITs, I still got admitted to a government-run engineering college. My parents expressed mild disappointment at first, but their happiness at not having to finance a private school education became apparent with time. Years, as they are wont to, passed. I emerged from tech school not knowing much about computer engineering, my chosen stream. I was lucky, however, to immediately make it to a prestigious management school, from where I eased out, after two years, into the *real world*. I settled in Mumbai with a high-paying job and had a couple of serious relationships (one of them was with a Catholic girl, and that had nothing to do with why we broke up). I started forgetting about the scarcities that had seemed eternal during my growing-up years in Muzaffarnagar. I was becoming a different person: I discarded expensive phones after every six months, drove around in a Honda City, stayed away from political bickering on Facebook, learnt to eat things that I could not have imagined as edible only a few years back (beef, pork, oysters, crab, prawns – you name it), spoke with excitement about technologies that could change the world, reviewed restaurants as a hobby, made a trip to Europe and planned one to the Americas, etc.

My parents were happy with the palatable parts of all this progress, which were the only parts that I bared before them. Any positive nostalgia that I held with regards to Muzaffarnagar diminished after every visit, as I began to see it as a place that had stagnated, a place that was keeping dear its faulty notions of the world – basically a place unable to accommodate the expansions of my character.

Many of my school friends had had journeys similar to mine, settling into comfortable lives in big cities in India or abroad. Perhaps we all didn't want to remember Muzaffarnagar much, which must partly explain why my contact with my school friends was non-existent, although some of them had found me on Facebook and added me. It was due to those courtesies that, on a boring office day when I had all the time to scroll through Facebook, I noticed one Daanish Alam in my 'Suggested Friends' list. The profile picture was all black, so I checked our mutual friends and realized that it was *my* Daanish. I went to his timeline and saw that the profile picture had been changed that very day. It was December 6. It took me a few seconds to comprehend the gesture: it was the anniversary (if it can be called that) of the demolition of the Babri Masjid in Ayodhya. As I scrolled down, I gathered that he still lived in Muzaffarnagar, which was a surprise to me, for I had always thought that Daanish would join his brother in Dubai. Had his brother ever really been in Dubai? There were many posts on his timeline that could be called religious in nature. There was one in which he ranted – with much anger, it seemed – against the recent beef ban by the Maharashtra government. Seeing some of those posts unsettled me, for it was difficult to imagine the free-spirited Daanish I knew bothering to associate with such heavy things. But there was no doubt that it was him, for I then checked his photos and *saw* him. He was still handsome, although he had gained a few kilos (not unlike myself) and had also lost some hair. He was into taking selfies, and was clearly still fond of maintaining a good appearance. This made me smile warmly. But as I clicked to see another album, the very first photograph made me pause.

There was a woman in the photo, handing a child – about two years old – to Daanish, who was sitting on a sofa. The woman might be Daanish's wife, I thought, and the child might be his, too. But this possibility wasn't what had most piqued my curiosity in the photo. It was the awkward, one-handed way in which Daanish was preparing to receive the child's weight – his left hand was outstretched, while his right was stuck firmly to his chest. I clicked on to the next photo. It didn't show the woman, only Daanish holding the child on his left arm, his right hand stuck to the chest in exactly the same way as in the previous photograph. I moved further in the album. A photo showed Daanish sitting pillion on a Bullet, his left hand on the shoulder of a man who was preparing to start the vehicle. The photo had been taken from a side, and Daanish's right hand wasn't visible in it. I then went to the album that contained his selfies, and gave them a second look. Now I noticed that they had all been taken from a similar angle, with the phone held in the left hand. In some of the selfies, the right hand could be seen in the lower left corner, transfixed in the same position, like a dead thing that had been dead for a long time.

I shut my laptop and tried to remember how to breathe.

# *B's First Solo Trip*

B notices a lot.

He is walking down a narrow, dusty lane, one of the many branching off from the busier main road. The morning is bright, almost too bright, pushing Diu into an early siesta. On either side are two-storey houses silenced by the sunlight. Here and there on the roads lie fresh splotches of cow-dung, though he does not see a cow anywhere.

He takes a turn and his chosen hotel appears before him. Recommended by his Ahmedabad friends as Diu's best budget hotel, Hotel Herança Buesa, one-time Portuguese church, does deliver a good first impression. Its attractions: an ornate façade towards the east, topped by a spire, a clear sea-view from the southern edge of the property, and a barbeque on alternate evenings. One let-down is the white paint on the overall structure, which has peeled off in patches, creating archipelagos of brown on each wall.

In the vestibule, he is greeted by an obese woman dressed in a nightgown. Her face seems swollen. She has dishevelled hair, as if the result of some terrible dream that she has just woken up from. 'We are the family owning the hotel,' she informs B.

He enquires about the rate of the smallest accommodation and, upon receiving the answer, accepts it. 'I was a student in Ahmedabad,' he says. 'Just finished studying architecture there,' he adds.

'Hmm,' the woman says, entering his name into the ledger. She then offers to show him his first-floor room and leads him outside, towards a helicoid staircase leaning on the north wall of the building.

'I am little scared rooming Indian backpacker,' she declares on the staircase.

'Why?'

She skips the question. 'My name is Miranda,' she says.

The room is basic. The walls, painted a sickly green, are mildewed. He walks into the attached bathroom, sensing its inspection to be an expected step in the evaluation of hotel rooms. The shower is kaput, and the green paint on the wall behind is peeling like snakeskin. He returns to the room with no intention of complaining about anything. He doesn't know if he should have expected better.

'Barbeque in the evening today,' Miranda says. 'Winston, my husband? Super fish he makes. You must come. Very cheap too. All the foreign people come there, even from other hotels.'

He nods in acknowledgement and Miranda leaves the room, her heavy feet thumping the staircase. He sits on the bed, which squeaks in greeting. On a wall, he notices a large painting with plain scenery, composed of a mountain range and a river and some huts – all anomalous with Diu.

He will rent a bicycle and go to the beaches, he decides. But for now, he will take a nap.

At Nagoa Beach, under the uplifting sounds of the sea meeting the land, he congratulates himself on the solo trip. A scrappy poem begins to form in his mind: The cotton at the fringes of the sea caressing toe-nails / The shore damasked with lozenges tracing the recessions of the waves / Waves, please stop, don't fill the hollows of feet too soon, let there be a mark / Wet sand, what makes you breathe? / The horizon, that straight line far far away, what meets what there?

But he soon realizes that because he does not know how to swim, the setting is – to him – interesting only in sight and sound, not in terms of the *fun* that it can provide. The views of the waves, the horizon and the sand are all fine, the music of the waves is fine, the poetry that swerves inside him is fine too, and he will try to write it down in his journal in the hotel, but as he gapes at the tourists taking on the sea with confidence, swimming distances into the water, or looks far towards his right and notices the abandon with which the children of the fisherfolk gambol in the sea, their spontaneity with the elements, a bout of ill-feeling rises within him. Things become clearer: strands demand that he be poetic in their appreciation, look at them and marvel at the calmness with which they meet the noisy sea, but beyond letting his feet sink in the sand, or looking at a translucent crab walking diagonally and briskly on it, or watching the slow process of the setting up of fishing nets, there isn't much involvement that he can have with the scene. In fact, he is scared to go even knee-deep into the water, for he is alone and unsure if anyone will care to save him if he were sucked in by a deviant current.

He decides to turn back and wait at the hotel till Miranda's evening barbeque is fired. He cycles for a while, and then takes to dragging the bike beside him. White tourists cross him in either direction on scooters and bicycles. To his right appears a hillock on top of which, as is mentioned on a nearby board, is a 'Sunset Point'. He props the cycle against the thickets beside the road. Then he climbs the hill. At the top, the sight of the descending sun greets him. Looking at the marvellous view, he cannot help but think that the only good way for the sun to set is to set over a grey–blue sea.

There are benches at the Sunset Point and he sits on one. He tries to absorb the entire scene. How far can he see to the left? How far to the right? He lauds his decision of allowing himself the freedom to see the world. He grew up in tiny, land-locked Muzaffarnagar, a rough place where no one ever understood him. Education took him outside Muzaffarnagar, but there was never enough time to explore anything. All his excursions into the world till now had been guided – by parents, teachers, or friends. Now he's gone out alone – something he has always wanted to do.

Just then he hears some noise from behind his bench. A couple scrambling up the last stretch of the hill. They look newly married, here in Diu for the honeymoon. The man has a round belly fitted into a tight T-shirt whose strained fabric suffers a considerable depression at the area of the navel. He is belching repeatedly, perchance due to the alcohol. The woman, not drunk, is gaudily dressed in a red sari with excessively glittery borders. Her anklets make a low clinking sound each time she moves.

The couple, giggling, sit on a bench not far from his. He tries to ignore them and go back to his thoughts. But then they start talking:

'Look at the beauty, jaanu,' the man says.

'Oho, it is the sun only,' the woman says.

'Let's go to the hotel,' the man says, snuggling up to the woman.

'What will we do?' the woman asks.

The man replies in a badly modulated whisper, one that is clearly audible at B's bench. 'Arre, what will we do? We will do the same.'

'I'm tired. No,' the woman replies. Her protest is weak, almost like an invitation.

'Come on, yaar. We have come here to have fun only.'

Drunk and sexed-up, the man is oblivious to B's presence on the next bench. The woman, he realizes, doesn't care either. The couple has encroached upon his moment. He stands up. Only half of the sun-sphere has submerged as of now, but he cannot stay to watch the complete drowning. The couple, now aware of him, shift slightly from their cuddle. He turns and starts climbing down the hill. Halfway down, out of sight of the duo, he retches in a feigned jest, as if there is an audience to laugh at his expression. But there is no fun in it. He realizes that such an incident could have appeared comic in company, but now, in solitude, it only evokes a viscous ill-feeling difficult to ascribe to anything.

He reaches his bicycle and lifts it up. He jumps on the seat and pedals towards the hotel. For some reason, he thinks of the only girl he has had anything akin to sex with. She used to come to his hostel room in Ahmedabad and let him do everything except the final act. He eventually got bored of her and cut her off.

There are nine foreign tourists at the barbeque, deftly attaching a considerable amount of fish flesh to their forks each time they want a mouthful. B, the only Indian there, is struggling with that. He is, in fact, thrusting thorns down with beer. Brawny, hirsute Winston manages the barbeque, attired in a vest and Bermudas. Miranda does the serving, helped by her two adolescent sons who look like they would rather be elsewhere. Miranda is still in the morning gown, still with the stunned hair. She does not approach B for re-servings as frequently as the others, and he has mixed feelings about that.

It is for the first time that he is eating a barbequed fish whole, with spine and skin and other fishy paraphernalia. He has only had soft fillets a couple of times before, as served by the campus mess once a fortnight. Here, the almost-alive eyes of the fish and its open mouth with tiny sharp teeth are for him a bit too lively. Things might have been different, he reasons with himself, if he had been eating non-veg food since childhood, like everyone around him now. How vehemently his mother had refused to wash the utensils when his father had brought butter chicken home once. Daal and roti, sabzi and roti, daal and chawal, daal and chawal and sabzi and roti – these were the stock meals at home, and at hostels. All vegetarian, Indian style. He remembers the day when he first ate chicken in his college days, tentatively biting into a leg piece just to shed the veg tag, just to feel a queer sense of liberation.

He was never initiated into the art of forks and knives. To eat with his hands would be practical now, and would save him from swallowing thorns, but it is unimaginable, considering the people around. On some occasions, his knife makes a screeching sound on his plate, a noise that makes him clench his jaws. Whenever he senses someone looking in his direction, he ceases his efforts at the fish, looks in the person's direction and smiles, while his mind worries about the clearly messy contents of his plate.

There are conversations all around. Though there is no single group, B is the only one sitting alone. Some time back, a guy from Denmark asked him where he was from and he answered India, as if India was a country outside of Diu. The guy did not ask him a second question.

He finally decides to dump the plate, gulp down a beer, and force himself to sleep. He looks around to ensure that no one will notice him when he places his quite-full plate in the dish-bin that Miranda has placed in a corner of the lawn.

'Don't like it, eh?' speaks a voice from behind him. Startled, he turns around to see a white girl standing just behind his seat with a pint of Foster's in her hand.

'Yeah, I don't,' he replies.

'Well it's bad. Too thorny, actually.'

'Yes … actually, yes,' he says.

The girl's comment is a relief. He rids himself of the plate, throwing it into the bin.

'So … what do you do? You are Indian?' the girl asks.

'Yes. Just travelling after graduation,' he shrugs.

'Good. Me too. You want more beer? I am going to ask Miranda for a Foster's.'

'Sure. One for me too.'

❧

The beer soon makes them chatty. Katy is twenty-three, Australian, blue-eyed, attractive despite excessive freckles; she has a model's body with shapely hips and a slender waist; she has muscular calves that suggest sportiness; she is wearing a beige top and white shorts, and green Crocs in the feet, which look particularly awesome to him; she laughs heartily with her beautiful teeth; and she is very interested in India. They talk about 'the family owning the hotel', their 'crummy' (she says) idea of painting the place in white, and the nuisance created by the alcohol-starved Gujaratis who flock to Diu on weekends. He explains things to her: that Diu is hot and maybe the family wants to keep the hotel cool with the white paint on it; that Gujarat is a prohibitionist state because it is the homeland of the father of the nation, Mahatma Gandhi, who was indeed a very saintly man. Then she talks: of how Sydney, her hometown, is a cosmopolitan city with all races of people; how not all Australians can be thought of as descendants of the left-over prisoners of the British (in response to an 'awkward' question by him); how alligators are different from crocodiles; and how dangerous and difficult bushfires are.

Soon they are tipsy and their talk becomes sparse and stuttering, and she yawns, and faint sexual hope twinges somewhere inside him.

'Do you have a boyfriend?' he asks.

'No. Had one. But now I'm here. So no boyfriend.'

By now, most of the other tourists have dispersed. Winston and Miranda and their sons are nowhere to be seen. And B is hoping. Hoping that Katy will stay with him; that she will stay with him longer to maximize his chances of saying something that will effectively and finally seduce her and bring her to his room of squeaking bed and dirty green walls and an absurd hanging with grotesque mountains.

'Do you see those girls?' she says, interrupting his inchoate fantasies.

'The ones sitting there? In the corner?'

'Yes. Them. They are Iranians.'

'Really?' he feigns surprise.

'And lesbians. Iranian lesbian … Fuck, it even rhymes.'

Is she is thinking of sex, too? 'How do you know?' he says.

'They hold hands sometimes and … I mean … they are

just comfy, right? Too comfy. And what the fuck are two Iranian girls doing in fucking India?'

Two fucks in a single sentence. He follows it up with a fuck of his own: 'How the fuck do you know they are Iranian?' and reruns the sound of the word, as he has said it, in his head, to check if his pronunciation has been casual enough.

'I was talking to them before you,' Katy says.

The conversation halts. He doesn't know what to say next. His thoughts are melting, flowing down too many inclines. He looks towards the Iranian girls. Katy is right. They don't look like sisters or relatives. They look like touring lesbians, far away from their iron cage, using India's vastness to express their sexuality.

'So what are you fucking tonight?' the words come out of his mouth.

It cuts short another one of Katy's yawns. 'Eh, excuse me?'

'I mean … sorry … What are you doing now, I mean tonight? After this.'

'Sleeping?'

He feels the thorns in his throat beginning to prick again. Katy stands up from the cemented slab they have been sitting on and pats away the dust on her shorts. He, sitting, finds his gaze fixated on her ass, on how puffs of dust glow for a second or two in the yellow halogen light.

Katy turns, bending her knees and leaning forward to be at the same level as him. Her top dangles to form an elliptical opening into which he now leers. Her breasts are his focus – pale ovals held well by the scaffold of a pink bra, they seem cooler than the heat around them; and although he is aware that he should not be staring at what he is staring at, he does not look away, using drunkenness as a pretext.

'You want to go for a swim tomorrow?' Katy asks. He

doesn't reply. She rests her palms on his knees, and his hazy eyes finally venture upward to meet her blue, curious ones. She shakes his knees and asks again: 'You want to go for a swim in the morning?'

'Yes.'

'Good.' She smiles, then she stands up and goes inside the Herança Buesa building.

---

Lying on the bed in his room, B allows imaginary correlations between race and sexuality to convince him that a white girl is better than girls of all other colours. He nurtures admiration for the unabridged sexual confidence of the white girl. How puerile the diffidence of the Indian girl appears before it. And how incomprehensible.

Katy, he imagines, is away from all encumbrances to the expression of one's sexuality in the name of tradition, any unnaturalness with impulses. He tells himself that tonight she was tired and just didn't want to have sex, and if she wanted to, she would have simply asked for it and they would actually have been doing it right now, possibly on this very bed. She is on a six-month-long India trip, he recalls from their talk. Isn't this, the tenure of the trip itself, guarantee that, given that she is white and free, she will fornicate with a few men along the road? Surely she will not remain sexless for six months. Whenever she wants it badly, whenever the itch comes to her in its strength, she will jump at a decent-looking man and devour him. Will she only be interested in white men? Plenty of white young men touring all around India, all taller and fitter and more handsome and more experienced at sex than Indians. But then, wouldn't Katy have accomplished this by just travelling in Australia, or England, or America? Here she is in India, *interested* in the damned country. Of course, during these months in India, she will want to sleep with Indian men in all shades of brown, and let India happen to her. Physically.

In his head, the possibilities keep repeating ... that if Katy is in India for six months, she definitely wants to have sex with some Indians ... and that one of those lucky Indians could be him ... and that it didn't happen on their first night, tonight, only because she had grown too tipsy ... and that maybe it will happen tomorrow morning after the swim.

After the swim!

He jolts upright on the bed. He has said yes to Katy. To her plan of swimming. What will he do tomorrow morning? He cannot even bloody paddle.

His agitation grows. And added to the beer inside his belly, it makes him feel dizzy.

He rises from the bed and switches on the light in the room. In an instant, the pallid, depressive green of the room's walls surrounds him. He paces from end to end, feeling squeamish. His slanting shadow follows him. Brooding without answers as much as he is, the shadow irritates him, even scares him. But after a while, the beer makes peace with his digestion. He then switches off the lights and returns to the bed.

Deviously, his mind wanders into other areas, concocting other worries. It starts with a series of axioms around the concept of Australia: Australia is an island where everyone lives on the coast and everyone has to know how to swim; Australia is a land where people are generally sporty and adventurous, and love water sports like surfing. And through such axioms, there emerges a single theorem – that Katy is an expert swimmer, perhaps an expert surfer, and she will not understand, let alone like a man so artless and without skill, ignorant even of the basest practicality of staying alive in water.

But how could he have learnt how to swim? He was born and raised in land-locked Muzaffarnagar, and the only swimming he had seen as a child was when, travelling with his parents to his grandparents' town during summer holidays, the bus would cross a canal and he would see some village boys bathing buffaloes and some others thrashing against the water's flow for fun. Later, when he was fifteen, his family visited a relative in Mumbai, and he saw the sea for the first time at Juhu Beach. It was a sea overwhelmed by the crowd assembled along its shores, a sea almost in the background. The elders with him were more interested in the snacks they could have at the food stalls. It was then that he told himself that he would one day travel alone. And now here he is, eager to engage but also incapable; his small-town self an accumulation of scarcities in experience.

How would Katy react if he told her that he has never seen a swimming pool in his life (the tiny one in his campus doesn't count, for they never filled it with water), or that he has never set foot in the sea, or that he has never had sex, or that, quite simply, he has never before been to a place he didn't have to go to.

Between these thoughts, his eyelids become heavy. But his perturbation makes him fight sleep. He sweeps away thoughts of Australia and swimming. What will happen will happen.

Because there is another reason why he doesn't really want to sleep as yet. He wants to recall the sexual hope of the evening, to reconstruct Katy's beauty: how her blond hair seemed favourable to touches; how her narrow waist met her curved hips; how she walked, her hips swerving as if to a rhythm. He decides to get hard thinking of Katy; to release his millilitres before sleep. The night would be wasted if it didn't end like this; if all the anticipation he built up was to be forgotten and wasted in the vacancy of sleep. He has to make something out of it.

So he thinks and thinks of Katy's countless attractions. But it fails. Even when he fantasizes about them travelling together and engaging in a little fling. Katy, or the Katy of his imagination, proves enigmatically useless to the brief sexual purposes of his night.

Minutes stretch ahead, sometimes long, sometimes short, and he grows frustrated out of stroking his benign penis. Then sleep traps him tightly and doesn't let go.

---

In the morning, he is woken by a persistent knock on the door. He fears it is Katy. Sucking his teeth, devoid of inspiration, he thinks of unresponsiveness as a good response, hoping that Katy will understand that he is sleeping and go swimming alone. But it isn't her at the door. It is Miranda.

'Arre baba, open please. Breakfast.'

He breathes out. 'Give me a second,' he shouts. He puts on his jeans and approaches the door bare-chested. Miranda shrieks seeing him like that: 'Eii. Go and wear a shirt.' He goes inside the room and puts on his T-shirt. Miranda has already come inside with the breakfast tray in her hands. He looks askance at her and notices a scowl. She is mumbling something. She keeps the plate on his bedside stool and walks towards the door.

'I didn't order breakfast. Is it part of the package?' he asks, hoping that the question will placate her and, by starting a conversation, serve as an apology.

'No,' she says without looking at him. 'Someone ordered it for you.'

'Who?' he asks. The answer is already in his head.

Miranda, for some reason, doesn't seem to like the question; she turns at him with fiery eyes and says, 'That Aussie girl you trying to loot. Who else? I knew you were a bad man. And now you run naked in my church.' She hisses away, stomping down the staircase.

Since when did the hotel become a church?

The breakfast – scrambled eggs, two toasts and some black tea. Katy has ordered it for him, which means that she expects him to get ready in some time. What can he do to avoid this? Loose motions, fever, allergy from saline water – what can be his excuse? He doesn't want to go to the beaches. He saw them enough yesterday, to the point of getting bored. But for him it is difficult to say no to Katy, not on her face anyway. Perhaps he should just confess that he can't swim and stay on the sand.

He finishes the breakfast and lies down on his bed again. Within minutes, there is a loud clanking of the latch on his door.

'Yoo hoo. Morning!'

'Yeah?'

Katy enters the room, and seeing him flat on the bed, gives an exaggerated pout. 'You're not ready?'

He likes the pout. To him it conveys a connection. He jumps from the bed. 'Oh yes, just give me a few minutes,' he says.

'So see you downstairs in ten?'

Their rented cycles buzz along, sometimes side by side, sometimes one trailing the other. Swimming-wise, he decides that he should just wait and see what Katy is capable of. If all it really involves is a little dip in a knee-deep sea, why not?

'There!' Katy shouts, and starts pedalling faster. Down the road, far to their left, is the first beach. They race towards the final stretch. Katy wins. Upon reaching their destination, they leave their cycles among the short bushes by the road. Katy locks their back wheels together using the chain lock on her bicycle, and keeps the key in her backpack. This locking of cycles leads to a dirty thought in his head. She removes her clothes to reveal a black bikini. Two Indian men stare at them from the other side of the road. For the next minute, while she spreads her sarong at a spot shaded by a coconut tree, B has to try extremely hard not to look in her direction himself. But he does look finally. He sees Katy loosening the thin elastic strap of her lower bikini, and his eyes rest on the thinnest line of tiny hair which starts from her navel and stretches down the taut stomach and then slips under the black cloth.

'Wooh,' she shouts, then breaks into a sprint that ends straight in the sea. She disappears under the water for a few seconds.

'It's *amazing*,' she shouts upon emerging from the water. 'Come on in.'

He weighs his crotch before removing his shorts and T-shirt. For a second he mulls the dangers of the sea. Then he walks towards it. He wets his feet. Katy urges him to jump in, reasoning that the sea is very mild. He lets go.

The sea water. In his stomach, it feels like what it is – a non-potable, alien liquid. He splashes desperately, in panic, to seek an exit from the swerving-receding medium. And he hears her laughter. Katy is laughing! As if his travails with choking and drowning are a flimsy drama he is playing to evoke some seaside mirth. Suddenly, his feet touch the ground and he scampers shoreward. He emerges a bit from under the ocean, and as flushes of relief come to him, he scampers faster. Faster and faster till a mild undertow sucks his feet and he falls, face first, on the withdrawing waves. A million sand particles prick his face, especially around the eyes and on the edges of his ears. From here on, he decides to crawl; his palms are now gripping the shore.

And she is laughing!

On the shore, he lies on his back, aware now of the validity of his fears. Nausea clasps his belly. Haplessly he gags, but nothing comes out. When he is done, he looks at Katy swimming blithely, romping in the waves in delight. Under a large surge, she dives into the sea, using the momentum to surf towards the shore; then she walks back to the earlier point and waits for the next wave. This is sport for her. But for him this is risky sport. Life-threatening. Each time she takes the wave and disappears under the sea for a few seconds, he panics. What if she misjudges a trick and is sucked in a whimsical current? He cannot, will not, go inside the sea to save her. He lies on the sand, gaping at her actions with terror. He gauges the horizon behind her to check for any onrushing tsunamis. He knows this is ridiculous, that he is getting paranoid. Sharks and sea-snakes are conjured up too. From time to time, Katy looks at him and guffaws and her teeth look agonizingly white and shiny – a little larger too, somehow; perhaps because her mopped hair makes her face seem differently proportioned. She doesn't look beautiful to him then, although large parts of her breasts are visible every time she emerges from the sea. Her shoulders make him trip over the adjectives tender and strong. He wants to leave. Will he be wrong in leaving her here on her own? She doesn't need him to enjoy. She doesn't need him.

He stays, burping a salty gas every now and then. Thoughts of her drowned death keep him busy, though.

Finally, after fifteen or so minutes, the torture ends, and she comes out of the water with a 'wooh'. His fears instantaneously mutate into anger.

'Wooh. The sea does well,' she repeats, the grainy skin on her body dripping water. Her body, its musculature.

Katy dries herself and puts on her clothes over the wet bikini. He too doesn't change his underwear. Without sharing many words, they look around for a place for lunch, and settle on a dingy restaurant called 'Sun 'N' Shore'. Katy orders a grilled fish and beer. He feels cheated, as if her choice is infringing upon some accord signed the previous evening against eating fish. He orders an Indian meal – the most Indian meal he can find. Also, to vent his anger and to make her feel a part of his sense of betrayal, he doesn't order beer. He goes for Pepsi instead. He hopes his resentment is palpable without his trying too hard, with the little gestures that he has already made. But why is he resentful? What will that earn? What does he expect of Katy when she realizes that he is angry? Anyway, she doesn't look perturbed at all.

'Ah, the sea does well … and makes one hungry too,' she says, before pouncing on her fish with her fork and knife. He breaks his roti into little pieces and dips them into his yellow daal and green sabzi.

'You don't know how to swim?' she asks. 'And you didn't

tell me.' She laughs a long laugh, tapping him on the shoulder in between.

He chews his food. Swallows.

'Hey, you alright?' she asks.

'Yes,' he says, glancing up at her from his plate, flashing a brief smile and then looking down again, as if the meal were an overpowering vocation that doesn't allow any distractions.

Beer after beer. Three beers. Katy grows talkative, making the lunch slower than he wants it to be. He is done sooner than her and has to order a lemon soda. After a while, in which Katy talks about a long and passionate love affair with an Australian air force pilot, the lunch is over. He gets up from his chair hastily, feeling jelly-like in his stomach. The food was terrible. Lucky, though, that he did not order beer.

'Ah, amazing fish,' she says as she gets up and gives out a little burp. 'Oops. Sorry.' She guffaws again.

At her suggestion, they go back to the beach to 'have a nice walk' before another dip.

And so without any major incident, in the throes of a receding anger, the rest of the day trudges along for him. Only that the wet underwear dries out and the sand inside abrades some of the skin on his balls.

During their return, he notices the width of the seaside roads. Traffic is still non-existent, yet he prefers now to cycle not beside but behind her. What irks him slightly is that even she makes no effort to align with him.

He made no effort to speak to her after lunch, did not dip even his ankles in the sea. That she is less and less effusive and is keeping her enthusiasm to herself is noticeable.

So Katy … transformed in his eyes now. Her zing, which had only yesterday evening been a swirl for his senses, is now nothing more than an inane jest. There she is, a couple of metres in front of him, pedalling her cycle, displaying the contraction of her strong calves with each up-and-down. She has become what she is – a Katy; a pretty Australian; a pretty alien.

They return the bicycles to the shop they had rented them from. Katy looks at him only when necessary. Her relative quietude is an acknowledgement of him snubbing her since lunchtime. As they walk back to the hotel, silent and side by side, he makes an awkward excuse about wanting to roam around the town.

'Sure,' she says. 'Go ahead.'

'I'll probably see you at the hotel,' he says.

'It's alright,' she replies.

He walks through the streets of Diu then, in front of small, gaudily-lit shops. Slowly he forgets about Katy and the day. A sad feeling wells up inside him, and for the first time he acknowledges that solo trips might not be that much fun after all.

After an hour or so of aimless walking, in which he circles, twice, an uninteresting part of town, he feels hungry. He asks some shop owners for a good restaurant. It takes him fifteen minutes to reach the place most recommended: Tango Restaurant.

Inside, he sees the two Iranian girls from the hotel sitting at a corner table, opposite each other, as if on a date. He walks towards them.

The girls recognize him and are glad to have him join them. They enquire about his day with Katy. He is surprised that they know. It was Miranda who told them.

'It was okay,' he says. 'We went to the beaches.'

There is no more talk about this. He orders beer and egg fried rice.

He comes to know that the girls are Iranian–Americans. And since one of them talks about a boyfriend, he concludes that they are not lesbians. For some reason, these things make him think of Katy as stupid.

His beer arrives first and he takes a large gulp. 'I guess I'm done with Diu,' he says. 'I'll leave when I figure out which place to go to next. Where are you going from here?'

'Ah! Good question, actually,' one of the girls answers.

'I ask because I don't know where I'm going. I don't know where I should go.'

'Well, one can only go back,' the other girl says.

'Hah. What do you mean?'

'She means go back to Ahmedabad,' the first girl answers. 'Diu is a bit of a dead end, haven't you seen on Lonely Planet? Unless you want to see starving lions in the Gir Reserve.'

Dead end. He finishes his beer, then orders another one. The restaurant is dimly lit, and the light of a pale bulb gleams softly off their greasy table top. He feels tired. Outside, the night darkens, and the world moves forward minute by minute. 'Diu is a dead end,' he whispers to himself. 'I didn't know that,' he says.

'It's just how you say some things, right?' one of the girls says. 'How did you end up here?' the other one adds.

'I don't know. Someone at college said that they had some fun here,' he says. 'They said it's nice and quiet and there is cheap beer. I never thought what could be next. I don't plan that way.'

'Well ...'

'So, by going back you mean what?' he asks.

'Where did you come from?'

'Ahmedabad.'

'Go back to Ahmedabad, then. The entire country opens towards the east.'

'Okay.'

'You really didn't know where you'd be going next?'

'No.'

The girls laugh at this. 'Guess that's the sort of people who end up coming to Diu.'

⁂

The Iranian girls go to a party being organized by a set of foreign tourists. He senses he is not invited. He returns to the hotel and goes straight to the vestibule to collect the room keys he had deposited in the morning to allow the cleaning of the room. Presently, Miranda and Winston are standing there, and their cold stare suggests that something is wrong.

'We waiting for you,' Winston says.

'Really? Why? There is no barbeque today, right?'

'No, not that. Katy checking out fifteen minutes back,' Miranda says. 'And you drunk.'

'So?'

'So it means you made me lose customer,' Miranda says. 'You made me lose foreign customer. Now she will talk about hotel with her friends and no one will be coming here. She'll say Indian backpacker comes here. I don't like Indian backpacker. I told you.'

'You get your stuff and you check out,' Winston commands. 'I'm angry at you.'

'But why? I want to stay here tonight,' he protests.

'Not possible only,' Winston replies.

'You're pushing me out because Katy left?'

'Yes. And I'm not pushing you.'

Something in Winston's voice suggests that he can't be reasoned with right now. 'Okay. So how much do I owe you?' B asks.

'We're respectable people,' says Miranda, sobbing. 'We running this hotel for years.'

Her voice angers him. 'I'm sure you're respectable people. You're respectably kicking out a guest for nothing at all,' he says.

Winston doesn't like the sarcasm. 'You want to fight me?'

'I don't want to fight. But I want to say that I'm not responsible for any of your guests leaving.'

'But in the morning she order breakfast for you,' Miranda says. 'And now she is leaving even without telling you. And you go out together in the day. Meaning you did something wrong in the day.'

'That's bullshit,' he says, raising his arms in complaint.

And then, like a rabbit lunging at his face, he glimpses a flash of Winston's fist. He tries to duck it, but fails. Sharp pain sears through his right eye. He falls to the floor. Winston is abusing him, but the words sound like a distant gong. He is angry and wants to hit back, but knows that it will be difficult to stand up. He can't open his eyes.

'*Go*,' he hears.

He struggles to stand up and turns away, but Winston catches him by the collar and shouts 'money' into his ear.

His mind isn't really functioning. He takes out his wallet and pays the room rent. Winston keeps holding him by the collar and pushes him right up till the staircase. On the stairs, he regains some of his clarity. It is then that the humiliation strikes him. 'Give me half an hour to pack,' he manages to say.

In the mirror inside the rotten bathroom, he notices that his eye is already beginning to swell. His head hurts stupendously. He washes his face and gets into the room. While packing his stuff, he wonders if he should look for another hotel to spend the night. There is also the option of the night bus that goes straight to Ahmedabad. He has to go there anyway, so he decides that he should leave this stupid town tonight itself. He steps down the staircase slowly, and begins to walk on the narrow path that had brought him here. After getting to the main road, reaching the bus station takes him another ten minutes. There, he buys a ticket on the bus that leaves earliest.

Twenty minutes after he takes his seat, the bus is still waiting to fill up half a dozen or so seats. That is when he notices Katy stepping in and taking a seat three rows ahead of him. Of course, where else could she be heading to but Ahmedabad? He wonders if she has seen him too. If she did, would she acknowledge him? Say hi? Perhaps she is angry with him.

The journey starts soon thereafter. He finds that his reclinable seat doesn't really recline, which is terrible because the journey to Ahmedabad is long – twelve hours.

It is possible that Katy did not recognize him because of his swollen eye, he reasons. In another two–three hours, the bus will stop for the driver to take a chai break. The passengers will step down to stretch their legs. He will walk up to her then. But what will he say to her? Will she think that he got himself punched in the town? He decides that he will tell her that Winston punched him because of her. That it's all her fault. Perhaps she will sympathize with him; perhaps, at the end of this journey, in Ahmedabad, they will decide to travel together. He will take her eastwards, into the heart of the subcontinent, away from the ocean. That will be fantastic. There will be a whole country to traverse before they hit the sea again.

The hours move ahead, and B's head hurts more and more. The pain doesn't let him sleep. He looks at Katy, who is listening to music with her eyes closed. Has she gone to sleep? There is a man, sitting a couple of rows ahead of her, who is staring at her just as B is. The man is staring not at her face, but slightly below it. Is she wearing a revealing top? Suddenly B realizes that he is the same man he had seen at Sunset Point the other day. His wife is sitting to his left, her head placed on his shoulder. B feels a spike of anger towards the man, of the kind he has never felt before. He wants to punch him. He wants this guy to get a swollen eye. On an impulse, he rises from his seat and moves forward in the aisle. Just when he is next to Katy, the bus takes a sharp turn to the left.

# *Diwali in Muzaffarnagar*

It was the day of Diwali, around three in the afternoon. I was in the toilet, the common toilet between my parents' bedroom – only in name, because they haven't slept together for fifteen years – and the room that houses my ailing grandfather. I was masturbating thinking of Marie-Anne, and I was close. I was looking at her Facebook pics, the ones I had taken in a hotel room in Nusa Dua, Bali, when the call came. 'Little Bro calling …' it showed on the screen. I cut it and went back to my business. But then he called again and I had to swipe right.

'Bhaiyya …' my brother Kanu said. He was sobbing.

'What happened?'

'I had an accident. A little one.'

On the day of Diwali, I thought. 'Are you hurt?'

'No, but …'

There was a pause in which I pulled up my pants and flushed. The sound of the water receded slowly. A different voice spoke on the phone then. 'Bhaiyya, we hit a motorbike,' it said. This was Kanu's best friend, a thin, sickly boy named Arun.

'How badly?' I asked, washing my hands and looking into the mirror above the washbasin. I saw my upturned shoulder meet my tilted neck, the phone lodged in between. There was no alarm on my face.

'He is asking for money,' Arun said.

'Okay. So …' So pay it, was my immediate thought. 'How much is he asking for?'

'And he beat us, Bhaiyya,' Arun said.

'Hmm … I am coming,' I said. Nothing came from the other end for a few seconds, so I cut the call.

I got out of the toilet on my parents' bedroom side. Then it hit me that I didn't know where my brother and his friend were exactly. So I called back on Kanu's number.

'Where are you?' I asked.

'We are at the Circular Road chauraha. Near Soojdo Choongi.' It was Kanu on the phone now. Sobbing lesser than before. But wasn't he was supposed to get sweets and crackers from Shiv Chowk? Soojdo Choongi, where he was, was a Muslim village just outside town, in the direction opposite to Shiv Chowk.

'Sorry, Bhaiyya,' he said, anticipating my thoughts. 'Don't tell Mummy–Papa.'

I cut the call. I passed through the verandah outside the bedroom and entered the living room on the right, where my parents were sipping tea and watching Baba Ramdev's contortions on television. They never try any of that stuff themselves.

'Kanu is in trouble,' I announced straightaway.

The idea of going to my brother's rescue alone did cross my mind. But I was not going to be the one to fight on the road. And what if the motorbike guy turned out to be a Muslim? This was Muzaffarnagar. Riot-prone-piece-of-shit town.

'What happened?' Father asked.

'I think he crashed with someone. Not a big deal. But the man is asking for money now.'

'Hain?' my mother exclaimed, rising from the plastic chair she was sitting on. The chair fell to the floor. 'Is he all right? Where is he?'

'He is okay,' I said. 'He is at the Circular Road chauraha. Near Soojdo Choongi.'

'Let's go,' Father said immediately.

⁂

We took the other scooter, me riding pillion, my hands holding on to the spare tyre behind my back. I can only drive scooters which don't have gears, like the Honda Activa I gifted my brother last Diwali, the one that he crashed. It was a ten-minute ride from our house to the chauraha, during which my father and I didn't exchange a single word. But this was normal. Papa doesn't talk much. Except when he is drunk, which was happening on a daily basis that week. He would hide his liquor in the tiny storeroom beside the main bedroom, and after nine he would go there with a large glass. A couple of swigs, and he would emerge from the closet having shed the disappointment that his sober self felt with us. In his inebriation, he abused the Muslim *qaum*, recalling how during the recent riots he had had to stay awake with a loaded rifle in his hands. It was unnecessary, I could have told him; the rioting never really reached the town proper. But, well, panic and prejudice make one do things.

At the scene of the accident, we saw Kanu and Arun

standing timidly, their heads bowed. The scooter and the motorbike, perpendicular to each other, leaned on their stands. A woman dressed in an elaborately embroidered red sari stood next to the motorbike. She had her pallu over her head, and had tucked a small part of it into her mouth. No way was she the assaulter. But the pallu told me that they were Hindus, which was a good thing.

We inspected the damage. Mudguard to mudguard, it seemed. A little dent and a little bend on either vehicle.

'Where is he?' Father asked the lady. She stayed silent. 'Where is your husband?' he asked again. Again no answer from the woman.

I went close to my brother and saw fear in his eyes. I put a hand on his shoulder. He tried to shrug it off. Arun, meanwhile, smiled at me wistfully while pressing his head with his palm. I nodded to him.

We waited at least five minutes for the assaulter to arrive. He had apparently gone to say hello to a friendly policeman somewhere nearby. There ensued a small conversation with him, in which he explained how the crash was the boys' fault. Kanu and Arun didn't seem keen to refute anything.

The man asked for a thousand rupees to repair the damage to his motorbike. For a second I felt like reminding him about his mandatory two-wheeler insurance policy, which could easily cover such damages. But something told me it wouldn't work here in Muzaffarnagar. It barely works in Mumbai, where I work.

'But it doesn't look like it will need a thousand rupees,' Father argued.

'Bhaisaab, it is Diwali time,' the man said. 'My festival has been ruined.'

Father took out his wallet and checked – only a couple of hundred-rupee notes in there. He looked at me. I didn't have enough to make it a thousand either. It was clear that someone would have to go to a nearby ATM, for which I, badly needing relief from the situation, volunteered. I took Kanu's Activa, which gave no hint of having been involved in an accident.

During my five-minute round-trip, my feeling was one of helplessness. But I had no conception of how the situation could pan out differently. I was angry too – I didn't know why – at Kanu and our father.

When I returned, the man was not at the scene again. I tried giving the money to the woman but she refused to touch it. She was biting a different part of her pallu now. My father was looking away, a grimace on his face. We had to wait for a few more minutes.

The man came back and took the money from me without any expression. Then he turned, kick-started his bike, waited for the seconds it took his wife to mount it, and sped off.

All of a sudden, Father regained control of the situation. 'You and Kanu go home. I will drop Arun to his house and come.'

~

On our way back, I asked Kanu what he was doing with Arun on that side of town. He chose not to answer, and I chose to repeat the question in a harsher voice. I was still angry.

'I would have bought the sweets and crackers later,' Kanu said gruffly.

'Yes, but what were you doing with him?' I asked. I heard

something in the scooter rattle unpleasantly. 'Was he the one driving?'

'Maybe yes. Maybe not. So?' Kanu said.

'So? You let others drive the scooter I bought for you? You want me to tell Mummy–Papa?'

'You anyway tell them everything.'

I thought about this. Not true, actually. After the break-up with Marie-Anne, I hadn't told my parents that I still harboured hopes of returning to her, or her returning to me. They were content thinking that I had realised my mistake after four stupid years with the French girl, and would now settle for a traditional Indian girl. Presently, though, regarding my brother, I thought I would not divulge any further information to our parents. But I couldn't resist prodding him about Arun.

'So why did you let him tag along?'

Kanu didn't answer. We were not far from our house now. A slight breeze had picked up, and the wind in my hair made me forget the question. This was late October, and the afternoon air was cool and pleasant. Mumbai can never match Muzaffarnagar in this.

'I like him,' my brother said then. 'He was with me because we like each other.'

My mind circled for some time around the word 'like'.

In the house, we saw something we weren't used to – grandfather was sitting in the living room, watching a news channel on television. The volume was close to maximum.

Seeing us, mother started her monologue. 'He has created such a mess. Passed urine on his bed. I gave him new pyjamas and helped him get here. I am not going to clean the bed. Let your father do it. It's his father after all. For ten years now I have been taking care of this old man and none of your uncles has given us a penny. Your uncles have all made their mahals. And all your father has done is bound this old man to my neck.'

There was no risk of grandfather hearing any of this. The man was ninety-four, and had been edging ever closer to deafness since grandmother died, which happened the same year I was born, almost twenty-eight years ago now. I was sure he was not getting much from the news show either. But he could talk, argue, manipulate. He was in that class of oldies who have screwed-up bodily functions but irritatingly high mental agility. We were all tired of him. Even my father, I suspected.

'Congress is screwing this country,' he said then, loudly, as only a deaf man can.

It made Kanu laugh, which brought Mummy's attention to him.

'And what were you doing getting yourself into an accident?'

He immediately looked down to the floor. Wrong move, I wanted to tell him. He should have answered back, been aggressive. Now there would be a barrage of questions.

'Why do you ride so fast? You could have died, don't you know? There are so many rash drivers on the roads. You need to take care not only of your mistakes but of others' mistakes as well. Show me, are you hurt anywhere? Is the other man hurt? And how much did your father have to pay?'

'I paid a thousand rupees,' I said.

'Thousand rupees!' Mummy glared at Kanu, who shrugged

ever so slightly. 'When will you learn to respect money?' she shouted.

This was the worst thing one could say to my brother in those days. That summer, he had fared badly in the national-level competitions that determine entry to engineering schools, missing the cut-off for well-reputed – and subsidised – government-run institutions by some margin. This had led to him being enrolled in a private college not far from home, which cost my father a bomb, and also barred Kanu from the kind of freedom I had in my college time. He had to take a bus to college in the morning and had to return by another in the afternoon. I had a feeling that he attributed my parents' vigilance – their not letting him stay in the college hostel, for instance – to my having had a *firang* girlfriend, whom I had met when I was in a hostel in Bangalore, where she was an exchange student. Kanu quietly envied me as the suave brother who had extricated himself from the shithole that is Muzaffarnagar. But it was something that Kanu could never say out loud, for when our father would retire from his miserable government job later that year, Kanu's tuition fee could only be borne by me. Did I like this equation? No. Except perhaps for the fact that it allowed me an upper hand in domestic quarrels, which I had to face no more than twice a year, during the annual Holi and Diwali holidays when I returned to Muzaffarnagar.

Kanu, as expected, did respond petulantly to my mother. He kicked the vacant plastic chair next to the one in which grandfather was sitting. 'Money money money!' he shouted. 'Everyone in this house talks of money!'

Grandfather saw what happened, and I can bet that I saw a smile on his face. Maybe he even heard something. It was loud enough.

Mother hit her forehead with her palm.

Kanu blustered out of the room. 'You had no plans for me!' he shouted from the verandah. 'You didn't even *try* to get me into a better college. You only had plans for him, and he did everything by himself. You don't love me because you think I failed.' He suddenly squatted down and started crying in despair, or maybe pretend despair, with his head in his hands and all. 'I heard it the other day when Papa said that you two had me too late. You can't deal with this, right? You can't deal with my college and his retirement at the same time.'

'Even your grandfather can hear everything,' Mother said. 'Don't shout.'

'I am not shouting!' Kanu shouted.

Mother went to the verandah to provide consolation, the way mothers have to. But such consolation requires hugging, which requires touching the other person's shoulders. My brother shrugged her off the first few times.

He did relent finally. Though the rage didn't die down, and even as Mother had him in her arms, he kept howling.

'And this old man doesn't die. Hangs on and hangs on and hangs on. I want this man to die.'

Grandfather showed no signs of having heard that. I agreed with Kanu. So much of our parents' energy had been sapped by the old man, whose desire for even his kind of depleted life was immense. His ears hardly worked, he had trouble walking, and father definitely had to help him in the toilet. But he still retained his joie de vivre. Every Sunday, he would demand for food to be ordered from outside, and father would get him his favourite dishes. Neither I nor Kanu remembered ever being pampered this way by our father.

I guess it was this identification with my brother's feelings that made me go closer to them. I had to say something, but, unclear of my own feelings, I ended up talking of money. 'You don't have to worry about money, Kanu. That's between me and Papa. You just have to study hard.'

This was earnest advice. To study, to learn something about the world that could be used to earn some money – that was the only way to escape the pettiness of Muzaffarnagar. I got out by studying hard enough to get into an engineering school in Jaipur. Then I went further away by getting into a management school in Bangalore. Then I moved to Mumbai – for employment and to live with Marie-Anne in a city that was beyond my parents' reach.

But since his college hadn't given him the first exit from Muzaffarnagar, detailing how my own exit had been achieved could only alienate me further from my brother. It didn't help that he was only seventeen, with hormones gushing through him like drugs, a body of rage and urges.

'Griha yuddh,' Grandfather shouted from the living room. The literal meaning in Hindi is 'domestic war', but the term is used to refer to civil wars. There was something about Iraq on the television.

Mother and Kanu stood up. 'I am so useless,' Kanu said softly then. 'I cause so much loss.' Contrition following rage – this was a common thing with him.

Mother answered predictably. 'No. You're not useless. You're the star of my eye.'

Except the cacophony from the television, things calmed down almost instantaneously. Kanu washed his face in the washbasin in the verandah. Mother and I moved to the main bedroom, where I flopped down on the bed. She sat with her back against the headboard. Kanu joined us a couple of minutes later and lay down next to me, such that our bodies were parallel, with both of us gazing at the still ceiling fan.

I thought of the evenings with friends where Marie-Anne would accompany me, looking the best among the women. Our male friends would envy me. I would hold her by the waist and we would dance to slow tunes. I would smell Summer by Kenzo on her. The fragrance always made me delirious. Almost six months now, I counted.

Mother interrupted my thoughts. 'What is my life worth?' she said. 'What is my life worth if the two of you act like this? Talk like this? If you two are unhappy? I have done nothing else in my life except take care of you. Of all you men.'

I didn't turn to look in her direction. What she said was true, and a few years back it might even have pained me, but now I felt like asking her, 'Why didn't you do things differently, Mummy? You should have done something for yourself. Maybe we would have been better off.'

Kanu, meanwhile, had moved closer to her. I kept staring at the ceiling fan, but from the corner of my eye I could see them hugging. Roles reversed!

'Tarun,' Mother told me, 'you should be closer to your brother.'

'Do we have crackers for the night?' I asked Kanu.

'No,' Mummy answered for him. 'Where has your father gone?'

'He went to drop Arun home,' Kanu answered.

'I hope he goes to the market,' I added.

Just then, my cell phone started vibrating in my pocket.

I took it out and checked the screen. 'Love calling …' it said. It was a call I had been desperate for, for months. But lying on the bed now, with my mother and my brother looking on curiously, I realised that it was a call I dreaded as well.

I took the call without changing my position on the bed.

Marie-Anne wished me and my family a happy Diwali. I realized that this could actually be the only reason for the call. Then she updated me about her life. She was somewhere in Switzerland, at a place called Interlaken. She asked me if I would visit her, and said she would love it if I did.

'Yes. Maybe. I will let you know.' I didn't know what to say. The awareness of the geography of this phone call – from Interlaken to Muzaffarnagar – saddened me somehow.

I think Mother sensed my feelings. When the call was cut, she said, 'You wasted four years with her in Mumbai. You were miserable when she left. Why do you talk to her now?'

'She called to wish Diwali, Mummy,' I said. 'That's all.'

'This is not a small matter. I can see this is not a small matter.'

I rose up from the bed. 'Believe what you want.'

'She is white. European. Haven't you thought of how many men she must have had in these months?'

'Stop giving me this,' I said in anger. It was tough enough to deal with this question privately. I went to the adjacent room to escape any further talk about Marie-Anne. This was my brother's study room, and had been mine earlier. I busied myself with a carton full of books, one of the many I had hurriedly dispatched to Muzaffarnagar after

Marie-Anne left Mumbai and I was forced to move to a smaller apartment. They were all in this room, the cartons, all stacked below a cot.

A few minutes passed in peace. Then I heard Father enter through the gate that separated the verandah from the backyard.

'Did you bring the pooja material and the crackers?' Mother asked him.

'I didn't get the time,' Father replied.

'You didn't get the time! What happened?'

'Ask him,' Father said loudly, pointing towards Kanu.

I stepped out into the verandah.

Father then told us how Arun had vomited as soon as they reached his house. His head had hit the asphalt in the accident. There was no external injury, but he had needed to be admitted to a hospital. Definite clot in the brain. Father said that Arun would be under observation for a few days.

'It's my fault,' Kanu said softly.

Mother asked Father if he wanted some tea and he grunted his assent. Then he went to the living room and reduced the volume on the television, which roused my grandfather from his nap.

'I gave Arun's family two thousand rupees,' Father shouted from the living room. 'The MRI will cost them five. I had to contribute.'

'The CIA is behind the crash, Harbir,' Grandfather spoke aloud. 'They are behind all mischief.'

'Let me and Kanu go and get the stuff,' I offered.

'Yes, go,' Mother said. 'And slow on the roads, please.'

I started Kanu's scooter. It rattled loudly, but still worked. As I rode with Kanu behind me, I wondered how long it would take Mother to reveal to Father that Grandfather had pissed on his bed. And that she hadn't cleaned it.

During our excursion to Shiv Chowk, Kanu and I spoke only when necessary. He did show a marginal interest in the quantity of crackers we bought. Otherwise, we were both too busy with our own thoughts.

I was thinking of what it must be like to clean a urine stain on a mattress. Was it even possible? Papa couldn't afford a nurse or a maid or whoever to take care of such things. I could, but that never crossed anyone's mind. It seemed that only our parents were expected to provide for our grandfather's welfare. Kanu and I were not expected to do a thing; not even serve him food. We were only expected to do our things well. To study well, to marry well, to make our lives outside Muzaffarnagar, and to ideally avoid any unpleasant incidents too, if we could help it.

But would we be expected to do similar work when Mummy and Papa got really old? I tried to imagine cleaning my father's faeces. Or my mother's. It made me shudder.

It was getting dark outside when we returned. The scooter's front wheel was beginning to feel a little wobbly by now.

Mother was the only one in the living room. She was watching a soap – one where a large family was celebrating Diwali, dancing to songs and bursting crackers. Even the vamps had let go of their meanness and were enjoying the festival of lights. Inside our house, there were lit diyas in every corner. I hoped that we would act like the family on television for the rest of the evening.

Seeing us, Mother said, 'We haven't even done pooja and they are drinking. They try especially hard to displease the gods on festival days.'

I reached Grandfather's room, where he and Father each held a glass of whisky in their hand. Father asked me to sit on a chair. Then he poured me a drink.

I took a sip. This felt like a set-up.

Grandfather raised his hand and gestured to me to come closer, which I did.

'What are your thoughts about marriage?' he shouted into my left ear.

'I have no thoughts about marriage,' I shouted into his right ear.

He closed his eyes and nodded; I knew this was in disapproval. Then he looked at my Father. 'Harbir, I love Tarun the most among all my grandchildren.' There were ten of us – the grandchildren. I had eight cousins from four uncles and an aunt. 'And my last wish is to be alive for Tarun's marriage.'

Hearing this, I finished my drink in a gulp and asked to be poured another. It unsettled Father slightly, and I guess that is what I wanted.

'It would be best, Tarun beta,' Grandfather addressed me now, 'if you were to marry within the caste. Marry a Jat girl.'

This inflamed me. I wanted to say that I had fucked with a white woman more than a thousand times over the past four years, that caste didn't mean shit to me, that their world didn't make sense to me and it probably already didn't make sense to Kanu. And I wanted to tell my grandfather that his last wish should be nothing else but to die in his sleep, without pain.

But I stayed silent.

'There is a proposal from a very good family,' Father said.

'What kind of family?' I asked.

'Her father and her brother are top bureaucrats. In the Central government. Delhi.'

'You are not a top bureaucrat,' I said, almost instinctively.

'But you are a top MBA. They are very interested.'

I sighed. What else? I also thought about Delhi – if I lived there, I would be within my parents' grasp. Just three hours away.

Then Mother entered the room, following the script almost perfectly. She stood behind Father's chair, looking at me as if she were certain that I was on the cusp of a decision.

'What do I have to do?' I asked them.

'You have to meet her,' Mother said. 'At a neutral place. It's going to be easy. Just see if your thoughts match.'

Kanu also came in. I don't think he was part of the script. He probably just didn't want to be alone in another room. Get out of this shithole, I wanted to tell him. 'So when do we burst the crackers?' I asked instead.

'I don't want to,' Kanu said.

'Why?' Mother asked.

Kanu remained silent.

'Arun will be fine,' Father said then. 'He is under observation. Nothing will happen.'

'But still,' Kanu said.

'Don't you like girls?' I found myself saying. This shocked Kanu, and he stared back at me like he would kill me. The expressions on my parents' faces changed too.

'Let's do the pooja,' Mother said, trying to scuttle the suggestion I had planted. 'And you brothers are going to burst the crackers. There is no need to say silly stuff.'

'Pooja!' Grandfather shouted. 'Let's have the pooja.'

All of us then got out of the room and walked to the little temple that Mother had assembled just outside the kitchen. Father had to help Grandfather get there. Many twinkling diyas adorned the temple – all Mother's labour. The idols sparkled in the diyas' quivering light. Mother placed marigold petals and some rice in our hands. These pooja rituals were among my earliest memories of my family. But now the gods had little to give, and I wondered if any of us really believed that a prayer could answer anything. We anyway sang the hymns that every Hindu household knows how to. I glanced at Kanu and felt a pang of guilt for what I had done.

Grandfather spoke aloud when the last hymn ended: 'May such Diwali come every year.' We threw the petals and the rice on the idols.

Sensing the irony, Kanu gave out a little snort, and because I wanted to apologise, I looked at him and smiled. He just stared back.

This was the point when I decided that I wouldn't go to Interlaken, that Marie-Anne was a mirage that my world had to close its eyes to. I never spoke to her again.

Two days after Diwali, I would travel to Delhi to take a flight back to Mumbai. In Delhi, I would meet the girl whose family had members in the bureaucracy. She wouldn't impress me much, and I would tell my parents so. But even in this rejection, they would find a silver lining. I was on the right track, they would say. That I felt defeated, that I almost cried in front of that bemused girl – it wouldn't matter even if I told them.

Upon landing in Mumbai, I would receive another phone call from my father. He would tell me that Arun had died in the hospital. He would tell me that my brother was in a fit of rage and was throwing the Activa to the ground repeatedly.

Father would not say it, but I would know that he wanted me to come home.

# *Reasonable Limits*

I had that chronic neck pain that you get from working too much on the computer, but all else was fine, in the sense that I was doing okay financially and had a stable job and was fairly settled location-wise and all, yet all these things as a composite felt like a lumpy contradiction, feeding a kind of unwellness that felt close to boredom, while being clearly very different from boredom, so it wasn't a great time for me and I felt life wasn't really giving me what I wanted from it; so yes it was probably a bad time, yes, and I had some nomad-type friends who used to come to my house to spend a night or two, you know the smart You-Only-Live-Once kind of people who do not hold a job for too long and who do not worry about a house or an insurance and other such things, such friends; and these friends of mine would urge me, over drinks that were bought exclusively with my money, to do things like they did things, to let go and basically discover my physicality or whatever, be Rimbaud or whatever, to see the world as much as I could: but please don't do it from the balconies of good hotels, okay? et cetera et cetera, and after hearing my friends I would feel compelled to outline the advantages of my position, the merits of obeying the order despite criticizing it; I would defend my place in the world, the unique coordinates of my independence, my committed cultivation of a life of the mind, and in my excitement I would sometimes posit that a life of the mind could only be cultivated around creature comforts, at which my friends would start their giggling; they would giggle because my AC would be running and my refrigerator would be humming and my mutual funds would be ticking, yet I would be the one with the dead eyes in those nights, I would be the soul in stasis, I would be the weakest bulb on the tree, so to say, the gist of the system, if you may, and so I guess it is not much to reveal that whatever I said to those fuckers only made me little in their eyes, and instead of giving me the solace of what was, only led me back to the bleakness of what *really* was, which is not to say that I saw the bleakness as bleakness, as cent per cent bleakness, for that couldn't be possible, I mean I had a routine, I had work, I had to go to office five days in a week, I worked in a life insurance company, I wasn't doing badly there either, and the company was doing well, in fact, so the bleakness was not really as absolute as I make it sound, but some things had led to dark sentiments, for example there was that gnawing story, always, that horrible story I had heard at work, the story of blood on paper, the story that I'd been told by the guy from Operations, about the frequent blood stains on the document scans received by Ops, the story that this guy had told me one day just in passing, which he started by informing me how any life insurance application needs to be appended with a slew of customer documents which are all collected and stapled together by the salesman, which are all excessively stapled in multiple places by the salesman because he doesn't want anything to be lost in transit and then have to ask the customer for it again, which seems only logical, and so the documents come excessively stapled and then have to be digitized because it would just be unwieldy and unwise to rely on paper throughout the processing of any life insurance proposal, so the documents have to be sent to an outlet that can scan them all, a scanning vendor, an enterprise that hires people to de-staple the excessively stapled documents, an enterprise that gets paid depending on the number of sheets it scans per month, an enterprise that therefore incentivizes its own people on the number of sheets they can scan per hour, an enterprise whose employees soon figure out that using any tool other than their own fingers to de-staple a thick sheaf of documents is a loss of time and money, and therefore start using their own fingers for de-stapling as standard operating procedure, whose hurried fingers thus bleed as standard operating procedure, whose blood stains the sheets to be scanned as standard operating procedure, and so on it goes day after day after day after day after day after day after day and then again, and at this point of the story's telling the Ops guy got a gleam in his eyes and a shine on his balding pate, he was happy that he had scandalised me, and that was not a mistake, for I was scandalised, I was in fact hurt and scandalised, and he surely saw something in my eyes for he then tried to calm me by reminding me of the good work that I was doing, reminding me that my project – of giving each salesperson a mobile application to capture customer documents as images – would mean that there would be no scanning required, that if my project succeeded, there would be no blood on paper because there would be no paper necessary, and I was surprised because I hadn't thought that that was the real importance of my work, and for a few seconds I allowed myself to be happy, till I understood that with my success, not only would there be no paper, there would be no scanning vendors, which was the real logical reason why the company wanted me to succeed, to not have to pay those vendors, because stapling was anyway easy to avoid, the sales guys just had to be instructed to use easily removable clips for each file that they made, but when I succeeded there would be no scanning vendors and there would be no employees whose job it would be to de-staple paper, and all those people with their horrible fingers, who had done nothing in the big city but pushed their nails against sharp metal, would be out on the street with nothing to do, nothing to do other than showing their fingers to the sun and peeling the scab off them, and it was thinking of those people whose fingers knew only piercing and bleeding that I would be disturbed at my workplace, and this disturbance added to the bleakness that I've talked of, a bleakness that was also being contributed to, in part, by the fact that the story was after all a clichéd one – the well-worn, age-old story of how an advancement in technology must mean that some people fall into irrelevance – a story whose persistence was a bigger problem than the contents of any single version of it, and I did not feel guilty of my own participation in it as much as I felt frustrated in the face of the hard truth that even if I were to extricate myself from this particular narrative, the elsewhere I would go to would in turn bind me in a new way, impose on me another damning mode of participation, where essentially the same story would tap me on my shoulder and hand me my specific role in it; and on nights with YOLO friends it was this inextricability that I wished to impress upon everyone, my buttoned down inextricability and their happy-go-lucky inextricability, for there was never a doubt in me that they too were participating, their versions of youth also had a price, they too consumed and produced, they too had no escape from eating the things and wearing the things and drinking the things that someone somewhere was scraping their nails to get made, just as mine was making the things that would put that nail scraper out of his job, which meant that all in all there was no cosmically correct way to be on this earth, and all you could do was be aware of what you were really doing, acknowledge its painful by-products, and keep at it, and keeping at it was what I would be doing, for I wasn't a revolutionary either, I knew that living in Yellow Pages was better than living in the crispy pages of history tomes, so I kept at it and looked at possible absolutions, I looked for inspiration online and started reading Wikipedia articles at work, only to realize that the denudation of my soul played its role here too, veering me away from what may be called general inspirational stuff and leading me to historical articles, articles detailing the cruelties of the past century, articles that described the magnitude of pain humanity had delivered and endured, and needless to say the Holocaust cast the biggest shadow among twentieth-century catastrophes, which is to say that I read a lot about it, pondering grand theories about State-sanctioned torture and death, and I thought about small silly things as well, such as whether Holocaust studies today could cover a peculiar twenty-first century phenomenon which may be titled 'How extensive reading about the Holocaust impacts one's evaluation of the Contemporary Arts', which means that one can't really watch a well-made movie about the complications of romantic love after reading this sentence: 'The Nazis took in a batch of Jews, had them stripped, made them stand in adjacent rows, shot down the front ones from such proximity that a single machine gun bullet killed the entire row, then pushed the bodies in the ravine, covered them up with mud, stepped down to shoot at anyone still squirming, and then called the next batch in'; so it is not much to say that misery hounded me, to the extent that the faculties that help us differentiate between one thing and the other began to be filed away in my case, things began to lump into each other, such that the workers with the leprous fingers seemed to me no different from the murdered Jews, one suffering dissolved into another suffering, contemporary became historical and vice versa, and I starting having weird dreams, such as the one in which I found myself in a huge field of corn or wheat, in a desolate field of corn or wheat, where a silent UFO cleaved the sky, a restful UFO, and ki-ki-ki went my heart; I still kept my chin up, though; I drank with friends, found critical paths of critical projects at work, played my own powerlessness day in day out ... and there remained pockets of my life that I liked, even enjoyed, but the heaviness would always return, I would think of those bleeding fingers, or would end up reading a sentence like: 'The disposal of corpses was hard work and required managerial acumen', and there were no lasting distractions for me even in any dull love that I tried fostering with a couple of ladies, and I followed the war in Syria, I paid attention to all reports of sexual crimes in India, I watched YouTube videos of American mass shootings, I read the bigotry of reader comments on op-ed pieces, I ate a lot of pizza, and I shrank and shrank on some incomprehensible dimension, realizing that the world was an inferno with only a few cool mirages, that there was only pure danger in 'getting out there', that my friends were wrong, that my friends' favourite writer Kerouac was wrong too, that great Roman candles that burn magnificently actually just burn away, and we all need to find a bed, and for as much as possible we all need to follow the injunction of waking up tomorrow in our own bed, in our cocoons of peace and laziness; we can and should continue our hiding, if it is that.

## *Good People*

For Ankush and Taruna, married life had begun to settle into a pleasant routine in its very first month. On weekdays, Ankush left for office at 9 a.m. and Taruna began her work from home after that. When Ankush returned at around seven in the evening, they joined forces to cook dinner – something they were getting better at with each passing day. Of the four weekends that they had lived together in Mumbai, they had ventured out of the flat only once. That was when their mutual friend Amit had come to visit them on a Saturday and they had all gone out to have lunch at a nearby restaurant. Amit had an interest in photography, and on that get together, he had gifted them four large framed photographs from their wedding. On the Sunday that followed, Ankush and Taruna had tried to find enough wall space for the photos in their 600-square-foot flat. They were able to affix only the smallest one in the living room. The remaining three had to be packed away. 'What an effort,' Ankush had said, and Taruna had laughed in the knowledge that it was the most exertion that they had had on a weekend.

The other weekends had been times of blissful inactivity. They stayed at home reading – Taruna her classic fiction, Ankush his modern thrillers. There were no friends or relatives to oblige – despite having worked and lived in

Mumbai for six years by then, Ankush hadn't fostered any such relationships. This suited Taruna, for she wasn't the gregarious type. Friends like Amit sought her out, rather than the other way around. Having come from Delhi, she saw Mumbai as a city where she had to meet new people and make new connections, and somehow she preferred solitude over relentless socializing.

Working from home was new for Taruna, and she had mixed feelings about it. She liked how it was apparently free of hassle – no daily commute, no forced chit-chat in the office. But it also meant no easy collaboration, and sometimes she missed looking to her left or right to get ideas from other people. She also found herself with a lot of free time – something that could be pleasant or deflating, depending on her mood. She had always found herself busy in Gurgaon.

In her free time, Taruna sometimes found herself thinking of their honeymoon. Those four days at a resort in Lonavala were coalesced as a single experience for her, and often ran in her mind in a single piece. The times she and Ankush made love, when they whispered sweet nothings into the other's ear, or goofed around in the lawns, and even the sleeping hours – it all came to her together. But, apart from this general montage, there was a short conversation with Ankush that sometimes came back more distinctly than the rest – as if it stuck out from the overall smoothness of the memory.

The conversation had taken place on the final day of the honeymoon. They had returned from a short afternoon hike in the hills close to the resort and were showering together in the bathroom. Their nudity was making them giggle. Marriage had added a proprietorial element to how they viewed each other's body, and the change was both comic and erotic. Ankush started rubbing soap on Taruna's back, and after a few seconds Taruna realized that he had grown silent. She thought that he was getting aroused. Several times during the past four days, hilarity had led to lovemaking.

But it wasn't so this time. 'I've always wanted to ask a question ...' Ankush said. There was a note of hesitation in his voice. And he had stopped rubbing the soap on her. Taruna took the loofah from his hand and asked, 'What?'

'I've wanted to ask you. How exactly did he ... how exactly did that man abuse you?'

Taruna turned to look into Ankush's eyes. She couldn't see through the water falling at speed; so she turned off the shower. 'What made you think of it?' she asked.

'Umm ... nothing. Just that I've always wanted to ask you this question. I know it's not a nice thing to be curious about. Horrible thing, in fact. And if there is a better time to talk about this, you can tell me.'

'No, nothing like that,' Taruna replied, 'you're my husband now.' She felt good that they could talk about a difficult matter.

'So, what did he do?'

'Fingers,' Taruna answered. Then, with her voice taking a detached, clinical tone, she added, 'He put his fingers inside my vagina.'

Ankush nodded imperceptibly and then turned on the shower. After a few seconds, he asked, 'Once?'

'What?'

'Did he do it once, or repeatedly?'

'Many times. It happened over two months. It was the summer vacation. I was eight.'

'Yeah, I know.'

'What do you know?'

'That you were eight. You've told me *that* before.'

Ankush didn't ask anything after that. They rinsed the soap off their bodies, then dried themselves and stepped out of the bathroom. A heavy silence thrummed between them. They lay down on the four-poster bed, clean and smelling of soap, the bed's white sheets and the white curtains around them somehow deepening the quiet. Staring up to the ceiling and its faux-antique ceiling fan, Taruna wondered what had made Ankush raise the question. She heard him whisper something. She looked and saw tears on his cheeks. And she heard what it was that he was whispering.

*Bastard.*

Ankush was crying for her. He was cursing her abuser. To see that was everything for Taruna: no one had ever been so moved by her pain. She kissed Ankush's tears, and then his lips. He hugged her tightly and they stayed that way for several minutes.

It was in that embrace that the specificity of that episode dissolved in the general memory of the honeymoon. Now whenever it came back to Taruna, she couldn't help but smile to herself. There was that frisson of validation for having married a good man, a man who could be pained by her pain. It was the most novel among all her feelings in the past few days.

Although she had spared Ankush the details, Taruna had revealed the outlines of her big trauma to him on their second date itself. Not being ashamed of what had marred her life at the age of eight – rather, *since* the age of eight – was something she had coached herself into by the time she met him. She was scarred by abuse and was self-aware enough to know the depth of that scar. She also knew that, unlike her, not every victim was scarred, that there were some who just forgot about it, or even some who could laugh about it.

But Taruna wasn't the forgetful or forgiving type. She could not forget those knobby fingers, those cracked fingernails, the dirt under those fingernails. She could not forget the hair just below the knuckles. It had happened during the boredom of summer vacations, during hot afternoons when others in the family, including her parents, dozed.

Over the years, she had struggled against random associations that brought back the dark memories. She struggled against summer afternoons. She struggled against dirty fingers. She struggled against men in kurta pyjamas who kept their top button open. She struggled against the sight of tobacco drool. These things brought back images, and the pain reached across all those years to sting her present – often assimilating new objects and images for its future invocation, bent on broadening its net of associations.

Marriage, Taruna hoped, would end the struggle. She loved Ankush. With him, it seemed that a resolute happiness could finally fill the big fault line in her past. There had been joys in her life, even when her struggle had been at its peak. She wanted to acknowledge those joys as joys. When she thought of the honeymoon in general, or of that instance of Ankush's empathy for her, she was convinced that she would heal, that not only was there a good future waiting for her, but her past was destined to see an improved assessment from her as well.

Honeymooning where they had, in a resort not far from the weekend outpost of Lonavala, was not the initial plan. For a good period after the engagement ceremony, they had discussed the prospect of going to Iceland. Their phone conversations had been all about fjords and geysers and aurora borealis then. Ankush had even started incorporating some Icelandic murder mysteries in his reading list. The idea of visiting a cold country in January didn't daunt them. They had compared Reykjavik hotels online and, despite Taruna's advice to the contrary (she thought all research could be done through free online portals), Ankush had even bought the Lonely Planet for Iceland.

But it was clear even then that big money was going to be spent in the wedding. Taruna's father had remained adamant about hosting a no-holds-barred show for his army of relatives, even if that meant gravely depleting his savings. He was stubborn when it came to showcasing an *image* – and in that Taruna found him to be the stereotypical Delhiite. On Ankush's side, his father had died five years ago and his mother, who lived alone in a house in Muzaffarnagar, kept an open hand. For Taruna, there hadn't been much clarity regarding Ankush's finances before the marriage. She had feared that their mutual enthusiasm about Iceland would gloss over the financial burden that the trip would entail, and that the pinch to their pockets would be felt later. She had known she couldn't fund the two-week Icelandic honeymoon on her own, and felt it was tactless to plainly ask Ankush about his financial situation. They had never talked about money till then. Also, with the slow unravelling of the financial martyrdom that her father took pathetic pride in, which included splurging on all showy things in the name of wedding shopping, Taruna had begun to equate *expensive* with *unnecessary*. This had ultimately included Iceland.

The eventual four-day Indian honeymoon had been paid for by her. Manzia Resort was high-end, located a few kilometres outside the town of Lonavala, next to a water body called Pawana Lake. Their room – cottage, rather – opened to picturesque views on two sides. The furniture, the upholstery, the bathroom fittings, the bed and the curtains – everything was tastefully done. Each morning, they saw a late-January moon set behind the mountains in the west, and as the sun rose from the east, the lake surface slowly changed its colours – from grey to turquoise to blue. 'Postcard level,' Ankush was compelled to say more than once. They never once thought of Iceland in the resort or after that.

Ankush, too, fondly remembered the honeymoon, although his memory focused more on the sexual element. And since the bodily intimacy wasn't just restricted to the honeymoon, and had understandably seeped into their lives in Mumbai, Ankush's memory of the honeymoon was that of a highlight period in the already glittery early days of marriage. The conversation about Taruna's abuse had been filed away by him; he would think of it only if asked to (which was improbable). At work, he often found himself talking of a healthy turn in his lifestyle, to which his older colleagues responded to with patronizing comments. He didn't mind that. He, in fact, had begun to seek the company of colleagues who were married, and had begun to think of the unmarried people in his company as *juniors*. Already there were signs of weight gain, and on afternoons when he had little to do, he sat vacantly in his cubicle and wondered if he could even have that thing that most serious men possessed – a little bit of a belly. He had mentioned this to Taruna once, and she had jokingly reprimanded him for the decadent desire. But it was true that Ankush could afford some kilos, and he felt good that all his typical nutrition issues were a thing of the past.

Ankush loved Taruna. His own love had at one point surprised him, for, unlike with his earlier girlfriends, he had sustained a long-distance relationship with her – a Mumbai–Delhi thing – for almost two years. Their first meeting had been a chance incident, the kind of tiny miracle that all love stories begin with. It was at the birthday party of his social-sector friend, Amit. Ankush didn't even know Amit well, but for some reason he had chosen to go to the party that evening. Inside Amit's flat, there were a dozen or so people, and a heated argument was going on. A woman whom Ankush had never seen in this circle before was at the centre of it. That woman was Taruna, and she was arguing with Amit; their disagreement was about whether the issue of child sexual abuse could be thought of as lying within the ambit of the larger movement of feminism. Taruna thought it was natural to do so, while Amit's point was to let feminism be unencumbered with a *peripheral issue*. Ankush could see that Amit's smug manner was having an effect on Taruna. So it was a gesture of sympathy when he chose to side with her when asked for his opinion, even though he was unsure of his own position with regard to it all.

At any rate, the altercation was soon drowned out by other immediacies. There was good liquor available. When they eventually got talking one to one, Ankush discovered that Taruna was in Mumbai only for a short, work-related trip. 'That's disappointing,' he blurted out. Taruna smiled at that. She worked in a non-profit organization in Gurgaon, in 'the space of' (as she called it) sexuality education in schools. He introduced himself as a 'middle-manager in a fin-serv company, nasty bosses, slackening reportees – the shebang'.

They exchanged phone numbers in the most innocuous fashion possible, almost mid-conversation. Then Taruna talked about feminism again, how the movement could encompass the fight for the rights of the male child as well. Ankush nodded in agreement, noting the streaks of hazel in her dark eyes.

That first meeting laid the ground for everything that followed. They chatted over WhatsApp for a whole week, not taking long in confessing their attraction for each other. The flirting came close to sexting, and a couple of weeks later, Ankush found himself taking a flight to go to Taruna's place in Gurgaon. At that time, she was living in a shared apartment in an area called Sushant Lok. Soon, regular arrangements began to be made to spend weekends together. Ankush travelled to the Delhi branch of his company at every pretence; Taruna increased the frequency and duration of her engagements in Mumbai. Within three months of this to and fro, *love* became a reality. And a year after that, the question of marriage was raised. That question, too, quickly transformed from being an emotional hillock to being a logistical problem – the incorporation of hundreds of people in a series of ceremonies, with as few residual grudges as possible.

They had first met in December, and their engagement took place in the second October after that. By then, they had arrived at the conclusion that it would be relatively easier for Taruna to shift cities after marriage. It was an agreement that Ankush had had to work hard for. Initially, Taruna hadn't liked the idea. She was beginning to make a name for herself in NCR and wasn't sure about starting from scratch in Mumbai. Also, 'following the husband' didn't sit well with her. Ankush convinced her that it had nothing to do with 'that thing called patriarchy'. Her shifting to Mumbai was the most logical thing to do, he told Taruna. He also promised that they would shift to Delhi after a year or so, once he had gained a promotion and could hope for better opportunities in the city. The eventual shift to Delhi would also make sense for him, he assured her, as his mother lived in Muzaffarnagar, a town only three hours away from Delhi.

Taruna's firm was fine with her working from home. Her salary would, of course, be reduced to sixty per cent of the earlier amount. Once the decision to move to Mumbai was taken, it didn't make sense for her to pay the rent for the Sushant Lok apartment any longer. She shifted to her parents' house in Dwarka till the wedding. But this also meant that spending weekends with Ankush became impossible.

They met, in fact, only once between the engagement and the wedding. It was in late-November, when Ankush was able to craft an office trip to Delhi. The meeting took place in a Japanese restaurant in Connaught Place, where they talked about Taruna's struggles with ensuring that her abuser was not allowed in the wedding. 'Someone came home to talk about it; asked me to let it be,' she told Ankush.

'Who is this someone?' Ankush asked.

'A close relative. Shit, I don't want to tell you who.'

Ankush could guess why Taruna didn't want to tell him the name of that person. 'So, what exactly does that someone want?' he asked her.

'To let him come to the wedding,' answered Taruna.

'Why?'

'It would be awkward … his absence. Everyone would ask about him.'

'And what's your stand?'

'I won't budge,' Taruna said. 'I won't let that man be a part of my wedding.'

Ankush placed his hand on hers. 'I'm with you in this,' he said.

Taruna smiled.

'So, what about Iceland?' Ankush asked then, to change the topic.

'Oh yes, I wanted to talk to you about that as well.'

'You have the itinerary?'

'The thing is, I don't know if we can really afford it,' she said. 'You must be under some strain. I don't have much – being social sector and all – and I think an Iceland honeymoon will cost lakhs.'

The clear soups they had ordered arrived just then, and in the time it took the waiter to place the bowls on the table, Ankush realized that he had never once thought about how they would finance their trip to Iceland. It also dawned upon him that, in the back of his mind, he had always thought that Taruna's father would pay for it.

'It will be expensive, right?' Taruna asked. Ankush, embarrassed by his own assumptions, couldn't say anything. She didn't notice anything amiss in his expression, though, and continued: 'We will go somewhere in India. We can always do Iceland later.'

'Yes,' Ankush said now, looking down to the soup.

'I see how much my father is spending,' Taruna said, 'and all for *show*. I argue with him all the time, about this and that novelty that he buys into. Thirty thousand or so spent on pugrees the other day. Can you believe it? And imagine if we went for an exotic honeymoon. Big wedding, and then honeymoon pics on FB – Iceland and all. He'd get to boast about it, too. So let's go easy on the thing.'

'Alright,' Ankush said. 'We will save up for a year and then travel somewhere fancy on our first anniversary.'

'Yes, that's better,' Taruna said. 'And no sharing photos on FB, okay? How's the soup?'

Later that evening, on the flight back to Mumbai, Ankush thought of the Iceland affair, and was shocked by the intensity of his disappointment. He realized that he had made an error in investing so much mental energy in the honeymoon-in-Iceland idea. And that too based on an assumption that he was now ashamed to admit to himself. Subconsciously (he told himself that word), he had fallen into the notion that Taruna's father would pay for the honeymoon – and wasn't that criminal? On the plane, lodged as he was in a middle seat, he scolded himself silently. Yet, there was a part of him that answered from the other side as well. The question of dowry wasn't there in this wedding, it couldn't possibly be. He had talked to his mother repeatedly to ensure that she not raise even the slightest of demands – not even in the name of rituals – with Taruna's family. Apart from the obligatory dinner for the baraat, Taruna's father wasn't expected to do anything more. With such pliancy from my side, Ankush thought, wasn't Taruna's father's profligacy something that he had chosen for himself? And if the man was going to be profligate, was it really such a big crime to have expected that he pay for the honeymoon?

Conversely, Ankush also questioned the very expectation that the baraat be provided for. This tacit agreement – 'that thing called patriarchy' – was the crux of all conundrums. Perhaps, he thought, I could offer to contribute to the expenses. But the offer would have to be made secretly; and in any case it remained uncertain how Taruna's family would see it: they might think of it as disrespectful and demeaning.

So he decided not to do anything of the sort, and began work at killing all the fantasies that he had built up about Iceland.

~

The festival of Holi was in late March that year, just two-and-a-half months after their wedding. It was customary in Ankush's family for the new bride to spend her first Holi in her father's house. So, train tickets to Delhi were booked. The day after Holi, they were to go to Muzaffarnagar to spend two days with Ankush's mother, and then they were to return to Mumbai via Delhi.

One Friday, about a week before their scheduled travel, Ankush came back from work to find Taruna in a terrible state. Her eyes were swollen, darkness beneath them, and her face carried a pained expression. She didn't have the energy for their usual hugs and kisses.

When he asked her what had happened, Taruna couldn't answer immediately. She exhaled, as if in great fatigue, and moved to the bedroom from the living room. Ankush followed her there.

'Is it about work?' Ankush asked. 'Things will start moving; it's just that this is a new city.'

'It's not the work,' she replied.

'Then what?'

'The Bastard.'

Ankush didn't grasp who or what this was about.

'I'm talking about ... you called him by that name on our honeymoon.'

His confusion stayed another moment. 'Oh, what about him?'

'He just won't die,' Taruna whispered, and started crying.

'Hey,' Ankush proceeded to hug her, 'tell me what happened.'

Taruna told him that the Bastard had had a heart attack and that he had been transferred from her uncle's house to her father's house. Apparently, her uncle couldn't afford the doctors and the care, and moreover, he had to go to a pre-scheduled stay at a vipassana ashram.

'Bloody vipassana is just a pretence,' Taruna continued. 'Now my father will have to take the burden. And after all that the man did to me.'

'Can't your father refuse?' asked Ankush. 'Can't he just say "I don't care"? Whatever?'

In response, Taruna just looked at him questioningly with teary eyes, as if he had suggested something silly. After a minute of silence, Ankush spoke again: 'If you don't want to go home for Holi, you don't have to.'

'No,' Taruna said. 'I want to go. Your mother also wants me to go. We have bought the tickets and everything; so there's no point not going. I will go. It's my home, after all.'

Ankush nodded. He wondered how Taruna's parents would manage keeping the Bastard out of Taruna's sight in their three-room flat. He would want the Bastard out of his sight as well.

'He can't move,' Taruna said. 'And he's taken my brother's room. So we won't have to see him, if that's what you were thinking.'

'Okay, that works,' Ankush said.

Taruna started sobbing, and as Ankush proceeded to embrace her tighter he, too, felt a helplessness clasp him. Then he heard her whimper something. She was cursing, saying 'fuck fuck fuck ...' Coming from her, the word sounded strange to Ankush. A moment later, she started shivering in his arms.

In the run-up to the journey to Delhi, Taruna tried hard to conceal her sadness. Ankush was trying hard too: he would come from office with a snack or some special dessert; he would play peppy songs, coax her to dance with him; he would wake up before her and fix her bed tea and breakfast. Taruna played along, and at times the simulation resulted in actual happiness.

Soon the day of their departure came. They took an auto to Borivali Station, from where they were to catch the Rajdhani. The decision of buying train tickets had been an easy one: both of them found overnight train journeys more comfortable than taking flights. During their courtship, when one of them had to make the journey to the other's city, they had travelled by train whenever time permitted.

They had been allotted the two side seats for their journey. Once inside the train, they pushed their two travel bags below the seats, and then Ankush placed the three framed photographs – which they'd decided to take to their homes – on the upper seat with care. They were offered tea and snacks almost immediately after that. Biting into their kachoris, they shared a comment about the sameness of the evening snacks on the Rajdhani. Taruna then remarked that this was their first Rajdhani trip together. After the snacks, they took to reading: Taruna her Dickens, Ankush his next instalment in a Nordic detective series. What lay ahead in Delhi was on their minds and, as the train sped, they sought their private distractions and stopped talking to each other.

Every now and then, one of them would look outside the glass window – but evenings still came early in March and there wasn't much to see except the unilateral rush of grey shadows. For Taruna, the shadows emerged into vision and vanished behind her; for Ankush, they popped out from behind his back and sped into a distant nothingness. On the one or two occasions when they both looked up from their books at the same instant, they shared a smile that had strains of conciliation in it. It confused them equally – conciliation for what?

They finished dinner early and were looking to stretch their legs even before the train reached Surat. Ankush jumped onto the upper berth after Taruna had helped him spread a white sheet on it. Soon, they were both supine, released from the weight of each other's company.

Taruna now thought of what lay ahead with greater intensity, and the past soon began pressing down on her. In her pre-teen years, even after the fact of the abuse had come out, Taruna's parents would expect her to meet and greet the Bastard cordially. She remembered how, when she entered teenage and became more sexually aware, the disgust she felt on such *cordial* occasions had increased. She had started touching herself when she was in Class XI, thinking of Hollywood actors or a classmate whom she fancied. But sometimes, the fantasies she would indulge in to arouse herself were cut short by a memory of the violation. Her urge would then collapse for days. Around the same time, she became an extremely difficult teenager for her parents – one who was always angry, always quick to pick a fight. Once, when she was seventeen, her father had asked her – ordered her, rather – to 'forget about it', to 'come back to normal'. 'You are stupid!' she had shouted back at him.

As an adult, too, Taruna recalled now, she had initially found it difficult to express herself sexually. Her first few boyfriends had all been unsure of her attraction towards them. It was only in her mid-twenties, after she had gained a specialization in child psychology and started work in the area of her choice, that the grip of her traumas had loosened. Rounak came into her life after that, and became the first man she had intercourse with. Then she dumped him for no reason at all. By that time, she had started dictating terms to her family, rejecting any gatherings of which the Bastard was a part. If her parents tried to cajole her, she would put her foot down.

'It isn't my shame; it is his,' she would say. This wasn't a concept that had come easily to her. Her folks would often respond by saying, 'You don't have to make it ours, too.' These were entreaties, and Taruna faced them with coldness.

She had been harsh to her parents over the years – harsh and inconsiderate, even in matters that did not concern that man – and, lying down as she was now, this fact hit her with force and nearly made her cry. The illusion of strength she had cultivated had to spill over to all her dealings, but did that also mean that she was condemned to keeping appearances one way or the other, always having to act tougher than she was? And how difficult it must have been for her parents: to know at every step the pain that was giving form to their daughter's mind. Her tantrums had been tolerated more than her brother's; her boyfriends had been well received; she had always worn whatever she had wanted to. Given who her parents were, Taruna couldn't deny that these were concessions. They knew she had to save herself, and they did try to accelerate that saving. But they also judged its progress badly. That was the sum total, and now that monster was inside her home. She closed her eyes, wanting to sleep. It's not my shame, she told herself again.

On the berth above her, a relieved Ankush had been scrolling through his phone. He was comfortable in withdrawing into himself now, with the knowledge that the whole affair would pass in a day.

He had read some articles about sexual abuse in the previous week. There were some damning statistics, but there were also some interesting takes on the whole thing. The philosophical question, which he believed he had rather smartly comprehended, interested him: At what age can a human being be thought of as being in control of their sexuality?

Thinking about the question vaguely again, Ankush was suddenly transported, by a not-so-indecipherable logic, to his first sexual experience. It was something that he hadn't thought of in a long, long time, perhaps more than a decade. He was twelve when it had happened, and the girl – his neighbour's daughter – was the same age. Her name was Gunjan, and in his memory, she remained a strikingly beautiful girl, the exception of whose beauty Ankush did not grasp entirely in his childhood. It was a hot afternoon in Muzaffarnagar and, away from the scrutiny of elders, they had rubbed genitals, without removing their clothes, in the shade of the lemon tree behind the building in which their families lived in adjacent flats. The exertion had led to his first orgasm, a dry one, and he still remembered how the weight of sin had crashed on him as soon as that was done. He had slapped Gunjan and accused her of making him do it. She, enraged, her cheeks flushing red, had pushed him back hard and run away. Afterwards, the incident became a huge ball of fire between them, making it impossible for them to even nod to each other ever again, which was difficult because, apart from being next-door neighbours, they were also in the same class in the same school.

Throughout his teenage years, though, Ankush had on countless occasions recalled the incident beneath the lemon tree to aid his private needs. He had fantasized about the passionate ways in which they would approach a repeat of the rendezvous, if there was ever to be one. In fact, Gunjan had remained part of his fantasies even after his family had left the residential colony for the house his father had bought in the town. It was only when he left for college that she withdrew from his mind.

The sound of someone's snoring interrupted these reminiscences. He sat up and looked for his water bottle, which had shifted from where he had placed it. As he moved, he noticed a definite tension in his crotch.

He had a gulp of water and kept the bottle in its overhead slot. He lay down again.

Their rubbing in the shadow of the lemon tree wasn't a crime, he thought. He was a child then, so was Gunjan, and children are curious about these things. Nor was the recalling of the incident for masturbation a crime. Teenage is a tough time; one latches on to anything for release.

But could he tell Taruna about this semi-erection that he had now? It wasn't the image of the girl-child that had aroused him, but the memory of the incident and the erotic connotations it had carried for him for a certain period in his life. It was the memory of being aroused that was the reason for this arousal. But was such an argument defensible? Had he really not reconstructed Gunjan just now in his head?

He shut his eyes and tried to force himself to sleep.

They entered the apartment at around ten the next morning. After the usual pleasantries with Taruna's parents and her younger brother, Ravi, were done, they went into Taruna's old room, to *freshen up*. The Bastard was locked in another room: gladly, they didn't see him.

Once inside the room, Taruna hugged Ankush tightly. It was a gesture to break the general air of silence that had built around them in the train. But it was also a gesture that affirmed that such a thing had existed. They kissed, lightly.

Later, while having breakfast on the dining table in the living room, with his father-in-law and brother-in-law giving him company (Taruna was helping her mother in the kitchen), Ankush's eyes fixated for a minute on the closed door of the other room, inside which the Bastard probably lay dying. The thought that the nasty old man might be aware of his presence discomfited Ankush. Then he looked towards his wife, working in the kitchen. How wrong would it be if a slice of bread toasted by her ended up going to the man?

After breakfast, two of Taruna's cousins – Akanksha and Avantika – turned up at the door. Ankush's presence apparently meant that it was a special Holi for them. Everyone, including Taruna's parents, moved to the rooftop of the building. Ankush remained a favourite target for colour-splashing, a role he took on sportingly. Taruna's brother Ravi once put ice cubes inside his shirt. Taruna saw this as the most carefree gesture the two of them had shared till date, and it made her happy to see the two most important men in her life come closer. In the raucous enjoyment, Ankush and Taruna's recent inhibitions were also shed. Soon, everyone was drenched and painted beyond recognition. Group photos were taken, as if to commemorate the disfigurement all of them had accepted for the day. In the hustle-bustle, Avantika's mobile phone fell in a bucket of coloured water while she was trying to take a selfie. Miraculously, the phone showed no signs of malfunction after she took it out. 'Holi Hai,' everyone shouted in unison.

But the group's energy was expended by then. Soon, the cousins left. 'You guys are old, but we have more Holi to play for sure,' Akanksha announced before leaving. Inside the house, Taruna went to the bathroom adjacent to her room for a shower. Ankush sat on the floor in the room, waiting for her to finish. He heard scraps of conversation from the living room. Taruna's parents were arguing. The Bastard had fallen in his bathroom while they were celebrating upstairs. Ravi was trying to calm them down. Then Taruna came out of her bathroom and it was Ankush's turn to bathe. 'There is an argument,' he told Taruna before going inside.

By the time Taruna dressed and got to the living room, there was no argument. She saw only her mother, busy with something in the kitchen. She had grown bulkier since the wedding, Taruna noticed. To help her in readying vegetables for lunch, Taruna proceeded to clean the coriander. 'What happened?' she asked her mother after a while.

'He fell in the toilet,' she replied.

'So?'

'So?' Taruna's mother turned to face her. 'What do you mean, so?'

'Nothing.'

'Your father had asked Ravi to check on your grandfather,' her mother said, returning to chopping the tomatoes. 'He just got too excited playing Holi with you and Ankush.'

'Does he need assistance while going to the toilet?' Taruna asked.

'He doesn't need to be washed, thankfully; he manages to do that himself. But it's better if someone lends a hand in helping him sit on the pot.'

'Disgusting,' Taruna hissed.

'Don't say that. That's how old age is. That's how our old age will be, and I hope you and your brother can at least help us sit on the pot.'

'You know I won't say the word when you or Papa are old.'

Her mother said nothing to that. When the coriander was clean and cut, Taruna walked into her parents' bedroom, where her father was doing something on his laptop. He hadn't cleaned himself well, and parts of his ears and neck still had dark-green colour on them. It looked ugly.

'You haven't washed well,' Taruna said.

'It will go in a couple of days,' he replied.

'Sometimes it can take longer. Just looks bad.'

'Hmm ...'

'Why don't you keep an attendant?' she asked him after a pause. 'Ravi can't be burdened with caring for him.'

'Your brother is not burdened with caring for him.'

'Why don't you hire an attendant for *your* burden, then? For mother's?'

'It costs money,' her father said. 'We will hire an attendant when we can't do without one.'

Taruna sat down on the bed, by her father's stretched legs. She placed a hand on his knees. Her mother and Ravi came in too, and sat next to Taruna's father.

'Ravi doesn't have to sleep in that room,' Taruna said. 'He can sleep in my room, with me and Ankush.'

'Don't be silly,' her father said. 'What would Ankush think?'

'He knows. He will understand.'

'I don't mind sleeping in the other room,' Ravi assured Taruna. 'And it's just for a night anyway. I usually sleep in your room these days.'

'Knows what?' Taruna's father asked her. 'What does Ankush know?'

'He knows what that man did to me,' said Taruna.

'Are you stupid?' her mother was scandalized. 'Why did you have to tell him that?'

'Why not? I'd told him months before marriage.'

'He's a nice man, Ankush,' her father sighed. 'But such things do no good.'

'Oh come on, you two,' Ravi stepped in. 'It's alright if she told him. It's good, even. He's her husband and she can tell him what she wants.'

Their parents shut up. Taruna whispered a thank you to Ravi.

---

At lunch, Ankush and Taruna sat side by side. There was cordial passing of bowls and chapattis. Taruna's father received a call from her aunt, who informed him that Avantika's cell phone had 'finally stopped working'. Everyone laughed at that.

Amidst the laughter, Taruna's father said loudly, 'So good to have my kids home.' He said it for no apparent reason.

Ankush noted his own inclusion in 'kids'. He couldn't help but think of his late father, who had died in a road accident. He had been fit all through his life. In comparison to Ankush's father, his father-in-law could be called portly, and that too would be underplaying the extent of his girth.

'Job-shob is going well, beta?' Taruna's mother suddenly asked Ankush.

'Yes, Mummy, it's going well,' he answered. He was conscious of using the words Mummy and Papa for Taruna's parents. So was she – they'd talked about it; and the awkward necessity of it was ridiculous to both.

'Any chances of shifting to Delhi?' she asked.

'No, not immediately,' he replied. 'I should get a promotion this year. It will be easier to find a job after that.'

Taruna's father then cleared his throat and said, 'It's better for everyone if you shift here, beta. Your mother lives not far from here, and Taruna can be closer to us too.'

'We're still only a two-hour flight away,' Ankush shrugged.

'Papa, even if Ankush moves here, he is likely to get a job only in Gurgaon,' said Ravi. 'They are still going to be two hours away from us, considering the traffic.'

'But it's still better for me if we move,' Taruna joined in. 'My office is in Gurgaon.'

Ankush gave a quizzical look to Taruna, as if to say, *We have talked about this*. Taruna looked back, *But it's true*.

'You like the sabzi?' Taruna's mother asked Ankush. 'Lo, take more.'

'But in Delhi you will definitely have better food,' Ravi added smilingly. 'Taruna's cooking is not the best in the world.'

'For your information, we cook together,' Taruna answered. 'And when you get married, you should cook with your wife, too.'

'So, when are *you* getting married?' Ankush then asked Ravi.

'Me? Oh, not any time soon!' came the reply.

The conversation continued in the same general direction for a while, with Taruna's parents asking Ankush to 'find someone suitable' for Ravi. Taruna too wanted to join in this hilarity, but she could also see the fakeness of it – a lightness that her family was assuming for Ankush's viewing. They wanted to be the gregarious happy family in front of him. Her parents were keeping up appearances, like they had always felt compelled to do. After this lunch, one of them would have to go up and feed that man his khichdi or porridge or whatever it was that he took at this time of the day. It disgusted her that that demon was behind a door right in front of her eyes; that he was breathing, snoring, farting, hanging on to life with the nourishments that her immediate family, her most loved ones, felt obliged to offer him.

'What about his food?' she asked the table.

'What?' her mother exclaimed.

'I asked – what about *his* food. When does he eat? What does he eat?'

'I will take the food to him after we are done,' her father responded. 'There is no need to bother Ankush with all this.'

'Papa, you know that he knows,' Taruna said, looking at her father with slanting eyes.

Taruna's father looked down to the table, unable to find the right words in his shame. Taruna caught Ankush looking at her with wide eyes, as if terribly surprised. Her brother had a stern expression on his face, while her mother seemed to have been further tired by the situation.

'Why is the truth such an inconvenience?' Taruna spoke, louder this time.

'Are you done with your little test?' Taruna's mother said to her in exasperation.

'What can we do?' her father said, addressing Ankush. 'We don't respect him, but we can't let him die on the street. We have to live in a society, right? What would anyone do?'

Ankush didn't say anything, mixing his well-mixed daal and chawal.

'There are nursing homes,' Taruna said. 'Dying homes. The poor also die.'

'Look, beta,' her father continued to address Ankush, 'you should try to explain the situation to Taruna. How can we *not* support him? That would be wrong. He is my—'

'Wrong?' Taruna shouted. 'That will be wrong? And what *he* did was *not* wrong?'

'Yes it was, beta, it was,' her mother rose, reached out to Taruna and hugged her. A tear ran down Taruna's face, but she wasn't crying. She was angry.

Ankush didn't know if it was proper for him to speak right now. And what could he have said? He understood his wife's anger; but he somehow felt that her father's voice was the more reasonable one. Why couldn't Taruna just let it be for now?

'It's a matter of a few weeks,' Ravi spoke then. 'He will die soon. Then it's all over.'

'I hope he dies today,' Taruna said.

'Don't speak like that, beta,' her mother said. 'Don't speak like that. It's festival time. No one should die today, not even a bad man.'

This seemed to calm Taruna. But the mood on the dining table had changed irrevocably. When Taruna's mother offered ice cream, her father grunted a no and went to their bedroom. 'I must have some ice cream,' Ankush said to lighten the mood, and stood up to fetch it from inside the refrigerator.

He was rattled by Taruna's last utterance, wishing an immediate death to her grandfather. He'd never imagined her as someone capable of throwing a death wish like that. When he returned to the table, he felt that he had to call out this aberration in his wife's behaviour. He served her the ice cream and, taking back his position, gently said, 'Why don't you just let it be?'

Taruna glared back at Ankush, slammed her spoon on the table, and walked away towards her room. Ankush looked to the other two people on the table.

Taruna's mother sighed, 'We're all good people here.' Then she put a spoon of ice cream in her mouth in the most tired way there could be. 'But how difficult it is to be good. How difficult.'

Taruna lay on her bed, dejected at hearing her husband utter the same words that she'd heard from her loved ones for most of her life. During their honeymoon, when Ankush had cried for her, she had understood him as an exception, someone who would staunchly stand by her side, always. She had hoped that he would not suggest a truce, like all the others.

*Let it be.* How could others ask her to let it be when they couldn't conceive what she had gone through?

Taruna considered it lucky that the abuse was exposed early. Her mother had happened to ask her if any adult had touched her *down there*, and Taruna, in her childish innocence, had detailed all that had been happening. Theirs was a joint family then, kept together by a business concern that the Bastard ran. There was one income source for all, and the man had total control. The revelation had led to a fight among the family members, with the Bastard claiming that his sons would starve if they left the house. Her father took the big step of moving his wife and children to a rented apartment. He had to find his feet anew, which took time. Taruna remembered how they had had to restrict their expenditures for a couple of years after leaving the joint household. To some extent, she had felt responsible, even culpable, for all that. In her childhood, there had been times when she had felt that it would have been better to say nothing to her mother, to *let it be*.

Ankush entered the room and lay down next to her on the bed. 'I didn't know you could be such a drama,' he said after a few seconds. They were both staring at the ceiling.

'I won't let it be,' Taruna said. 'I have never let it be.'

'Why did you tell your parents that I knew?'

'Has it ever occurred to you,' Taruna shifted to her side, now facing Ankush, 'how difficult it is for me to see my loved ones pretend, right in front of my eyes? How difficult it is when everything is shown to be perfect, all theek thaak?'

'Everything *is* theek thaak, my love,' Ankush said. 'I love you and you love me, and we got married two months back.'

'So am I the only sore spot?' Taruna asked.

Ankush turned towards her and hugged her. 'No,' he said. 'I said it because I thought it would be better for you.'

'I know, but ...'

They kissed each other on the lips.

'You understand that it is also difficult for me, right?' Ankush asked.

'What do you mean?'

'What am I to do with the weight of this knowledge? The man who raped you sleeps ten metres away from where I just kissed you. Your parents are providing for him. Your brother helps him do potty. You won't, rightly, let it be. What is to be done?'

'Nothing, I guess,' Taruna sighed. 'I've asked myself the same question.'

'Maybe I should kill him.'

'You know, earlier today, when you came out of the bathroom … I stepped out of our room for water. I went to the kitchen, and when I came out I saw him in the living room. I mean I didn't *see* him see him, I just saw his back and his legs. He was on a wheelchair, turned away from me, looking at the TV in the living room. My brother was behind him, apparently moving him around. I froze. Is he still curious about what's on TV, I wondered. Does he still want to live? It made me shudder.'

Ankush held her tighter. He wanted to force her out of this bleakness. But then, wasn't she just powerless before the spectre of her grandfather? He kissed her again, soft and long this time. But he did so while feeling miserable himself, stuck to the aftermath of an event that had happened a full two decades back. They didn't say anything to each other for a while, and in the silence, they both fell asleep.

---

They were woken up in the evening by Taruna's cousins, who had come over for some fun with Ankush jiju. Ravi also joined them, and soon it was decided that they will all play Ludo to pass the time before dinner. The game lightened Ankush's and Taruna's moods. During the game, the conversation turned to how much fun everyone had had during the wedding. 'The photographers had it really tough,' Akanksha said, 'everyone was pulling them over to this side and that.'

'Have they given the album yet?' Taruna asked.

'Tayaji must know,' Akanksha answered, referring to

Taruna's father, who had commissioned the photographers. 'Till last week they hadn't. That I know.'

'That's ridiculous,' Taruna said, rolling the dice. 'How can they be *so* late?'

'Yes, that's strange,' said Ankush. 'The photographer on our side gave the album in ten days flat. We will be seeing it in Muzaffarnagar.'

'Your photographer was here, jiju?' Avantika asked Ankush.

'No, he covered events on our side,' he answered.

It was Taruna's turn again. She found it improper that Ankush had referred to some events prior to the wedding as *events on our side*. Was the wedding itself not an event on *their* side? She rolled the dice, thinking whether she should say what was on her mind. Then she did: 'Probably your photographer could give it earlier because he was just a plain guy, not doing artistic stuff. Ours is an expensive wedding photographer. That sort of thing takes time, no?'

'I'm sure, yeah,' Ankush said, taking the dice from Taruna's hand. He didn't know how much his mother had paid the local photographer in Muzaffarnagar, but he knew it wasn't much. The photographers at the wedding were paid by Taruna's father, and he remembered how they had conducted their business far more professionally. What Taruna had just said was the truth, but it still made him uncomfortable. Had Taruna just accused him and his mother of being cheap? Should they have offered to share the photography expenses in the wedding? He didn't know the answers, and he believed he couldn't have possibly thought of these questions before the wedding. And now the deed was done. He felt guilty for not being world-weary enough to catch such a mistake while it was being made. And he felt angry at Taruna, for bringing it up only now.

The game ended soon after, with Ankush and Taruna both losing by a margin, largely because they found themselves in a pattern in which they cancelled each other's progress. 'Your album isn't here, but we have other albums in the house,' Avantika said. 'You want to check out some old albums, jiju?' she asked Ankush. 'Sure,' he answered, and they all walked out of the room. In the living room, Taruna's parents were having tea. 'So how are you guys enjoying?' Taruna's father asked. 'We are going to show the old albums to jiju,' Akanksha answered. 'Good idea, good idea,' he mused.

A stash of old albums was taken out from a cabinet inside Taruna's parents' bedroom. The first one that they took out had photographs from Ravi's sixth birthday. Taruna's cousin turned the pages excitedly, telling Ankush who was who. Ankush responded with customary surprise while noticing the difference in appearance many people in Taruna's family had suffered over the years. It was fun to begin with.

Once in every seven–eight pictures, there appeared a figure that neither Akanksha nor Avantika would pause at. Ankush understood that it was him, the Bastard. He had a round body, a lot of face fat, and it seemed that there was always paan drool on his lips. But the fact that the cousins also glided over those photos, that they never paused to explain who that man was – it was disconcerting. It provided for the possibility that the whole family lived under the shadow of a single truth, and was still struggling to confront it. Taruna betrayed no emotion, but Ankush felt helpless nevertheless. He calculated: the photos were from Ravi's sixth birthday, so it must follow that Taruna was close to nine at the time. The incidents had already happened. He then paused at the next photograph in which Taruna appeared, looking closely at the child's face. There was much of the future Taruna in that little child; he could see that in the facial features. But he couldn't shake off the feeling that it was a robbed child he was looking at. It made him sad, and when he looked up at Taruna, he carried the sadness in his gaze. Taruna saw him looking at her. She pursed her lips, said, 'Some of the pictures in this album should be thrown away.'

Ankush nodded slowly. Why hadn't her parents already done that? Why such lethargy, considering the convulsions this man had caused their household?

'I will take care of that,' Ravi said and kept the albums back.

They came out of the bedroom and saw that Taruna's mother had prepared tea for all. She called Ravi to the kitchen to take a thermos of hot water to the room where the man was.

Sitting in the living room and sipping his tea, Ankush realized that he could not now forget the face he had seen. He knew that an older version of that face was inside the other room – grimacing, wilting, edging towards death.

'We should check the photographs we brought, too?' Taruna said to him.

'Which photographs?'

'The ones Amit gave us.'

'Oh yes.'

'They are from the wedding?' Akanksha asked.

'Yes.'

'Cool, let's see them.'

After finishing their tea, they went back to Taruna's room and unpacked two of the three large photo frames diligently. The glass was cracked on both.

'Fuck,' said Taruna. 'Fuck.'

'We took care in the train,' Ankush said.

'All the shit has to happen together,' Taruna said.

'It's only a frame, guys,' Ravi said. 'I'll get it fixed. Let's find a spot for these.'

'We will use this room only, na,' one of the cousins said. 'It's your room, didi.'

Taruna moved her hand over the third one, which was still unpacked. 'This one seems alright,' she said.

'This is the one that we were planning to give to my mother,' Ankush told Ravi.

'Yea, this is the one,' Taruna confirmed.

'We can hang this one here,' Ankush said. 'And give one of the others to my mother on our next trip.'

'No, no, what's the point,' said Taruna. 'We will take it to Muzaffarnagar as planned. Ravi will get the other two redone for here.'

On Ravi's proposal, Ankush agreed to some drinks that evening – beer, basically – and it was arranged that while the two would accompany everyone at the dinner table, they would have only some starters and then eat their food later in the night, after their drinks. Despite Ankush's request, Taruna's father excused himself from the session. His wife answered on his behalf: 'Beta, alcohol gives Papa acidity. You young ones go ahead, please.' For Taruna, there was a bottle of rosé wine in the house, and she promised to have a glass with the boys after dinner. As for the cousins, they were deemed too young to be offered alcohol.

Taruna was glad that the cousins had stayed back for dinner. Although she had disliked the carefree, jovial airs her parents had unsuccessfully donned earlier in the day, the prospect of another energy-sapping conversation at the dinner table was too much to bear. The cousins would make that impossible, she knew. And any serious talk she wanted to have with her parents could now be had when Ravi and Ankush would be drinking beer in the other room.

At the dinner table, the conversation began, understandably, with the wedding. Some new anecdotes were shared. 'Some of the baraatis were jaahils, by god! Only interested in dancing. As if they had never heard music before.' This was Akanksha. 'There was one, you know, who was teasing me,' Avantika added, 'so I poured water on his plate of food when we were serving the baraat. *Good* lesson he got.' Taruna's father felt the need to admonish them: 'You shouldn't have behaved badly with our guests.' 'But Tayaji,' Avantika protested, 'it was *they* who were behaving badly.'

Ankush didn't like this talk – not because he was offended by the jokes made at the expense of the baraatis, but because of the semblance of a method being followed even while making this small talk. He knew for certain that the drinks session that he and Ravi were supposed to have was planned well in advance.

'Well, jiju, the marriage-sharriage was all fine,' Akanksha now nudged Ankush, but where exactly did you take our didi for the honeymoon?'

Ankush smiled back at her vacantly. Then he looked towards Taruna, hoping that she would provide an explanation on his behalf. She offered him no expression.

'It was Lonavala, wasn't it?' the younger one now asked. 'I've heard the place is closer to Mumbai than Mussourie is to Delhi.'

'What, jiju? We were all thinking that jiju is a corporate hotshot and all. That he will take didi to Europe-shurope and all, and you two went to Lonavala! Tch,' Akanksha said with an exaggerated pout.

Ankush looked towards Taruna again. This time, she gave a little shrug. 'Well, that's how it turned out,' he answered the cousins.

Perhaps his tone wasn't even when he said that, which is why his mother-in-law asked the cousins to shut up. 'That's a matter between them both,' she chided the girls. A couple of giggles later, the honeymoon talk died down.

But Taruna's father started something else now. 'So, in your company, Ankush beta, what is the highest position that you can attain?'

'There is of course the CEO. I'm six levels down,' Ankush answered.

'And how much does the CEO earn?'

'I don't know exactly. But one point five, two, two point five crores? Maybe more,' Ankush said.

'Anyway, how many years,' Taruna's father asked, 'might it take you to reach that level?'

Having predicted this question, Ankush chose to answer with a cruel degree of exactitude. 'Several years. And given that not everyone becomes a CEO, the likelier scenario is that I'll never become one.' After a pause, he turned to the cousins: 'So Europe-shurope might always be difficult, hain?'

In a gesture of taking up the awkward challenge that Ankush had thrown to the table, Taruna's father spoke first: 'You should develop a savings habit, then.'

This time Ankush checked himself for rudeness. 'I do save, Papa,' he said in a conciliatory tone. 'I save some each month. Ask Taruna.'

Taruna nodded towards her father with her eyebrows raised. She was swallowing a morsel.

'And where do you put your money?' Taruna's father continued.

'I buy mutual funds. Mostly. Or an FD every now and then.'

'Mutual funds are good – good for medium-risk investing. But individual shares are where the real money is made.'

'That's true,' Ravi chipped in. 'Papa had some pharma company shares once that gave like 300 per cent return in six months. Right, Papa?'

'Right,' the father-in-law said. 'I get these tips from some of my friends. They always work out fine. It's all about putting the right capital in at the right time.'

Inevitably, as it seemed to him, Ankush thought of his serviceman father. Thoroughly risk averse, the man was suspicious of even mutual funds, always favouring simple savings products from the national banks that he held his accounts in. Ankush knew better; he surely managed his money alright. And his education had told him that anyone who professed mastery over the share market was a fool. If it was a place to make easy money, it was also a place where one could lose their life's work in a single hopeless hour.

'I'm not willing to move my mutual fund portfolio,' he addressed his father-in-law, 'considering that my CAGR has been a good 13 to 14 per cent.'

'CAGR?' Ravi asked.

'Compounded Annual Growth Rate. Yeah?' Ankush answered.

'Good,' the father-in-law said. 'That's very good.'

---

The cousins left soon after dinner. Ravi and Ankush went to Taruna's room and opened their beer pints. Taruna filled her glass of wine and only half finished it before moving to her parents' room, saying that she wanted to 'catch up with them'.

Ankush soon grew bored in Ravi's company. There was nothing that was common between them. Unlike Ankush, Ravi liked neither football nor detective stories. But Ankush sensed that they were different at a more fundamental level. While Ankush had left his parents' house in Muzaffarnagar at the age of seventeen, and had never since been in Muzaffarnagar for a stretch longer than a month, Ravi had, on the other hand, never left this home for more than a month. Not knowing how to strike an interesting conversation, Ankush took to drinking faster, and was down to his third pint inside half an hour. Ravi was still holding his first pint in his hand.

'Fuck, man,' Ankush said, slightly tipsy, 'you nursing a heartbreak or something?'

'No. Why do you say that?' Ravi laughed.

'I don't know. Just.'

'I don't have a girlfriend, but I'm not heartbroken either,' Ravi said.

'Hmm … so how's it like, taking care of that old one?' Ankush asked.

Ravi's face showed a momentary confusion. 'My grandfather?' he asked then.

'Who else?'

'I'm not really in charge of taking care of him.'

'Aren't you helping him in the toilet?' Ankush asked.

'Not really. Once or twice. Just holding him while he loosens his pyjama. Papa is the one who does most of the caring.'

'Don't you feel like shit doing this? After all that the man did to your sister?'

Ravi shifted in the small chair that he was seated on. 'I've always stood by my sister's side in her arguments with the family.'

'That's good to hear.'

'My father is a social man. It's his personality, you know,' Ravi's voice was a bit more sure now. 'He does what is expected of him. And in this case, what are his options, really?'

'It doesn't take much to kill an old man,' Ankush said. It was only after he uttered the words that he realized that he did, indeed, believe what he said.

'Are you really suggesting that?' said Ravi, his forehead scrunched.

'I'm sure you've thought of it,' Ankush answered. 'Haven't you?'

'Can't say I have not,' came the reply.

'And I bet your father has thought of it as well.' Ankush realized he liked being the provocateur.

'I am not sure of that,' said Ravi. 'You don't know my father enough. He's very correct, you know.'

'Can you pass me another pint?' Ankush said. Some of the conversation on the dining table hadn't felt *correct*.

'Sure.'

'Thanks,' Ankush said. He used the opener to remove the cap and took a large swig. 'And what about your mother? What are her views about the whole affair?'

'Apart from his food, Mummy has taken a vow not to do anything more for the man,' Ravi said. 'She doesn't want to see him, and I don't think she's had any need to till now.'

'That's because of Taruna?' Ankush asked.

'Yes. My mother hasn't spoken a single word to that man for twenty years now. It's really tough for her too.'

Seeing Ravi get emotional, Ankush held back his next question. The whole family was stuck up, he thought. He gulped down his beer then, and asked Ravi for another, which Ravi opened without question. It was Ankush's fifth pint inside an hour and he felt he was getting sick.

Just then, Taruna came into the room and asked them if they wanted to have dinner.

'What! It's just been an hour,' Ankush said.

'He's drinking very fast,' Ravi complained, pointing to the empty bottles lined next to a wall.

'I'm heating the food,' Taruna said.

After they were done eating, Taruna requested Ravi not to sleep in the other room. 'Bring in a mattress here,' she said. 'There is enough room.'

'If I feel any trouble, I'll come here,' Ravi said. 'It's just for a night.'

He left the room.

Taruna and Ankush prepared to sleep. In bed, Ankush took Taruna in his arms. 'So what did you discuss with your parents? Which shares should I invest my *capital* in?'

'No, not that,' Taruna said. 'Although it won't be too bad if you took Papa's advice and tried in a couple of shares.'

'What I don't understand is the … the … incorrectness of the conversation?' Ankush mused. 'He shows interest in my money right after your cousins tease me about the honeymoon.'

'The honeymoon talk shouldn't have offended you. They were just pulling your leg.'

'Maybe they were. But if it was a joke, then why was I the only one at the end of it? If the honeymoon location was so important for your family, maybe they should've paid for it.'

'You think so?' Taruna said.

'In fact, for a long time, I assumed that your father would pay for it.'

'Why?'

'Why? Wasn't he already spending so much? Your biggest worry in those days, remember? That he was overspending to make a show of wealth to his relatives. He could have spent a few more lakhs and gifted us the honeymoon. The show would have been complete. And, you know, my love, I really wanted to go to Iceland.' As he said the last bit, Ankush tried to snuggle into Taruna's neck. She pushed him away.

'Fuck off, man,' she said. 'You're drunk.'

'Yes, I am. But mostly fucked by your family. Why don't they tease *you* about not taking *me* to Iceland?' Ankush slurred. 'That would be proper feminism, right?'

'Please shut up, Ankush. Don't say stuff you will regret. Sleep.'

Ankush went to sleep in the next five minutes, but Taruna had many thoughts to keep her awake. The conversation that she had had with her parents rang in her mind.

Taruna had joined her parents in the bedroom after a hasty glass of wine with the boys. There, she had found her father on his desk, fiddling with his laptop; her mother was on the bed, leafing blankly through a magazine.

Taruna placed herself on the bed. 'Has he eaten?' she asked the room.

'He eats much earlier than us,' her mother replied.

'And sleeps earlier than us?'

'Yes.'

'What a life.'

'We are under a lot of stress already, Taruna,' her father said, angry. 'Are you always going to be sarcastic?'

'You should hire an attendant,' Taruna quipped.

'I told you that an attendant costs money,' said her father.

'Yes, and I'm wondering where your money has gone.'

'You don't know?'

Taruna knew. 'Papa, that's the thing! Why did you have to spend so much money on the wedding? I asked you not to, at every step I asked you. But you didn't listen. Your stupid Punju pride came in the way.'

'Don't talk like that, beta,' her father said, softening a bit. 'To spend for your wedding was my pleasure – my pride. It *had* to be done like that.'

'Tell me, how much have you spent on this? On the oldie? And how much more are you going to spend?'

Her father didn't answer. He acted busy with the laptop. 'Five lakhs, that's what the hospitalization cost us,' Taruna's mother answered for her husband. 'Now it's all the medicines. His heart is operating at 10 per cent; so, surgery isn't possible. This could drag on for a month.'

'How much more is needed?'

'Your father is already in debt, beta,' Mother said.

'Stop, Sheela,' Father interrupted her.

But she didn't stop. 'Every day that the man lives, it becomes worse.'

Taruna shook her head. She knew that her father had no income since his business had folded three years ago. He had otherwise been deft at managing his savings and assets, but the extravagance of the wedding had had its impact.

Her father was holding his head in his hands now. Taruna went up to him and rubbed his back.

'How much do you owe people?' she asked him.

'If it has to be done, it has to be done,' Mother said. 'There's no point in counting how much.'

'How much is it?' Taruna asked again.

'Three,' Father responded.

'How much more do you need?'

'Four. Maybe five. I can keep an attendant then. I owe this money to your mother's brothers. They contributed to the wedding too. That wasn't a loan, true, but I cannot stretch their generosity any further.' He wiped his eyes with his T-shirt. 'I can manage. I would just have to sell something.'

Taruna's first thought was what all this meant for her brother. Ravi wanted to set up his own design firm, and he would need some help from their father. Now she feared that the family might have to sell its assets in the near future, all because they were short of seven or eight lakhs in cash.

She sat on the bed, right beside her father's desk, and considered the situation. After spending a considerable portion of his savings on her wedding, for which he had felt the definite compulsion of tradition, her father was basically *done* with her. She could never ask him for any financial help ever again. Her *dowry*, so to say, had been dealt with. She knew that, in her father's mind, all that was his was now part of Ravi's inheritance. If this were some other family, she would have been critical of the mindset in which only the son inherits property. In her own family, though, her natural reaction was to not quibble about her share but to think of her brother's well-being. She hoped that when the time to help Ravi came, her father would have something left to sell.

'Why did you irritate Ankush with the share market and all? All this talk about where to put money. You've your own issues to handle, right?'

'If he felt bad, tell him I'm sorry. Though it's true that I can give him some share market tips. And everything will be alright; you don't need to fret.'

Taruna smiled wistfully. Then she said, 'Why don't you just kill the old man?'

Her father was silent. Then: 'Don't say stupid things.'

There was something about Life that had revealed itself to Taruna just then. Lowering your head and carrying on – that's life. Carrying on and finding solutions. But her father wasn't finding solutions – he was borrowing from his son's future to pay for his father's last ransom. Realizing this, Taruna felt a spurt of anger.

'You have screwed Ravi's future,' she mumbled. 'You've made him a house boy and you've fucked his dreams.' She stormed out of the room then, looked with rage at the closed door of the other room, and walked towards the room where Ankush and Ravi were having their beers.

Despite her anger, though, she'd understood that her father was in need of financial help.

A few hours later, Ankush woke up in sweat from a dream. He had seen himself investigating the murder of someone dear to him, although the dream hadn't allowed him to ascertain the identity of that person. There were no clues to be worked upon, and the crime seemed unsolvable. He was desperate; he saw himself scribble something excitedly in a small notebook; it was also something inconsequential, something unrelated to the crime, something the dream didn't allow him to see either, and something that therefore became a mystery inside a mystery.

When he had shaken himself out of the dream, he realized that he was thirsty. He heard Taruna's calm breathing, though once in every few seconds her lips pursed to let out a little whistle. How different she seemed now – different, vulnerable. She was his wife and she was another person: these simple facts achieved a certain magnitude in the moment. He felt a surge of affection towards her – an affection tinged with fear.

He checked the time on his cell phone: 2.30 a.m. He stood up from his bed and tiptoed towards the kitchen, where he gulped down two glasses of water. Coming out of the kitchen, he turned to look towards the other room, the one in which the Bastard was sleeping. The door was ajar and, out of a morbid fascination for what was inside, he approached it.

Inside, it was darker than the lobby, and he heard loud snoring before he saw anything clearly. Slowly, the figures on the bed gained shape. Ravi was on the far side, taking as little space as possible; and the Bastard, his face turned towards Ankush, was snoring spectacularly. The shrivelled old man who once raped a child, thought Ankush. He tried to stoke his hatred, but what was before him was only the vestige of a man. The face conveyed no trace of the evilness that Ankush's mind had imbued its earlier version in the photos with; and now, in its withered avatar – relaxed, rotting, eaten by age – it was the face of a man whose crimes were a long distance past him. Death was the only outcome waiting for him, and Ankush allowed himself the thought that the delay in this outcome was a kind of justice. For a brief second, he even considered if it would be good for Taruna to see the old man in his current state. She would not be able to forgive him, or feel that any semblance of justice had been granted her, but her malaise would at least erode a bit. For what retribution could be sought from a man sleeping on the rim of life?

Standing in the dim light of the room – fixed to a spot, breathing silently – Ankush also saw just how this *difficulty of hate* must be a problem for others in Taruna's family as well.

He stood in the room for a good five minutes. A part of him also wanted to discard the softness creeping inside him – softness for the old man, for the situation, for the family. The whole thing had been bogging him down for days now. The old man's death would relieve all the burdens, that much was clear. And perhaps, it seemed to Ankush, all it needed was some doing.

There was a chair next to the bed, close to where Ankush was standing. There were two cushions on that chair. Ankush considered smothering the old man with one of the cushions and ending the whole story then and there. It wouldn't make him a criminal, he told himself. This man had raped his wife when she was only a child; and now his wife wanted this man dead. Everyone wanted this man dead.

Ankush picked up a cushion carefully and pressed its fluff with his thumbs. He brought it closer to the man's face. It could be done. He could do it. But in the movies, the victims always thrashed about violently. Even the insensate ones thrashed about when denied respiration. It would require strength, Ankush guessed, and even then it was likely that Ravi would wake up and stop him. Realizing this, his tense muscles relaxed. The sweat on his forehead cooled. He put the pillow back and saw that his body was shaking, as if withdrawing from a fugue that the mind had forced it to enter. The best option was to go back to his wife. Tomorrow they would go to Muzaffarnagar and the situation here would be behind them. The man would die soon. It would all pass.

He turned and moved out of the room, taking care to close the door completely, for he knew that Taruna would wake up before him and that seeing the door ajar would upset her. He lay down next to her and kissed her lightly on the forehead. I would have killed the Bastard had Ravi not been in the room – with this thought, he tried to push himself to sleep.

Soon, he started dreaming again, and the dream now showed him as both the detective and the murderer. It was so confounding that when he finally woke up five hours later, his initial confusion was that his middle-of-the-night adventure had only been a dream.

The morning came to life quickly. Ankush had woken up with a headache and his mother-in-law gave him a lemon tea to help ease it. Taruna had black coffee. There was a quick breakfast that followed, where nothing more substantial than 'good morning' and 'how was your sleep' was said. Then the couple got ready for their journey to Muzaffarnagar.

A week back, Ankush had asked Taruna's father to arrange an outstation cab for the journey. He wanted them to travel in comfort, at their own schedule. There was no online service providing outstation cabs in Delhi at that time – none, at least, that he had not found to be overpriced. Taruna's father had booked a cab for them, and Ankush assumed that the rates were going be reasonable.

Just as they were about to leave, Taruna's father provided a little twist: 'When you reach Muzaffarnagar, Ankush, don't bother with paying the cab driver.'

'Why, Papa?' Ankush asked. 'We never talked about that.'

'He's a nice Punjabi kid, the driver. And he knows me well. I can settle payments with him later.'

Taruna saw this as another example of that self-harming impulse that plagued her father. It was an expense he could do well without. 'No, Papa,' she told him. 'We will manage, it's no problem at all.'

'There is no point spoiling him, beta,' said her father. 'He might charge you a silly rate.'

This told Ankush that his father-in-law hadn't discussed the rates with the cab service. 'You can help us set the rate downstairs, Papa,' he said. 'But I insist that I'll pay. It will become a bad habit if I take your offer now.'

It happened so. Taruna's father came downstairs to see them off. The rate he settled with the driver was only marginally better than the lowest one that Ankush had discovered online. Totally not worth the drama, Ankush thought.

It was a Tata Indigo. They piled their two bags in the boot and placed the photo frame carefully on the front seat. Then they sat on the rear seat and were on their way.

When they had crossed Dwarka, Ankush said, 'I now realize how adamant your father can be while trying to be generous.'

'You didn't discuss the rates with him on the phone?'

'No, I thought there was no need to state that explicitly.'

'That's why he assumed that you wanted him to pay.'

'I see.'

'He's like that,' Taruna said. 'He was like that at the wedding too. Arranged transport for many of the guests. He paid for a cab to go to Jammu and return to Delhi, just because some relatives had been too lazy to buy train tickets.'

'Wow,' Ankush said. 'We didn't pay for any of our relatives' transport.'

'Maybe the groom's side isn't expected to,' Taruna said.

'Is the bride's side expected to? For their own relatives?'

Taruna didn't answer and they didn't talk for a while then. She wondered if Ankush remembered the stuff he had said last night. If she didn't have something to ask of Ankush, she would have argued about all that now. Nevertheless, it bubbled inside her, and the restraint she put on herself made her irritable. She identified with those pathetic housewives who have to ask their husbands for money, and who are condemned to be calculative of the potential responses that could come their way.

The mid-morning sun strengthened and came in through her window. The rays made Taruna's skin sting a little. She wondered, for the first time, if it would have been better not to tell Ankush about her abuse. Asking him to loan some money to her father so that the Bastard could be cared for – that wouldn't have been difficult in itself. But now, since Ankush knew, it was like asking a husband to pay for his wife's rapist.

Taruna had swallowed this cruel irony last night. She had her reasons: she loved her family, cared for her brother's future. But why should Ankush be concerned?

It was Ankush who broke the silence after a while, when they were crossing Ghaziabad. The road was narrower and bumpier now that they had entered Uttar Pradesh. 'I think I said some silly things to you last night. I don't remember exactly. I'm sorry.'

'It's okay,' Taruna replied, instinctively. Ankush held her left hand and squeezed it. It was then that she recalled that it was not okay. Her restraints began to loosen in her mind.

'I must say your brother is a very straightforward guy,' Ankush said.

'It was about the honeymoon,' Taruna said.

'What?'

'Last night. You were talking about our possible honeymoon to Iceland.'

'Oh yes, your cousins had pulled my leg quite a bit.'

'Not that. You were talking about how you thought my father should have paid for it.'

Ankush just sighed in response. They grew silent again and looked out their side-windows. The grip of their hands had loosened. There was not much to see, though – some derelict shops and the ageing residential complexes behind them, covered in dusty air.

In Muradnagar, Ankush's mother called him. 'It was a great Holi, yes … Yes, we are on our way … It's two-and-a-half hours from here … We will stop midway for lunch, so yes, add another half hour … See you, Ma.'

'How is she?' Taruna asked after Ankush cut the phone.

'Excited to see us.'

'Look, Ankush, there is something we need to discuss.'

'I don't think we should discuss what I said last night. I was drunk.'

'No, not that.'

'So?'

'My father needs money. Can you give him a loan of three lakh rupees? Four, if you can spare that much. He will return it over the course of a year.'

Ankush shook his head, a look of disbelief in his eyes. Taruna found his reaction artificial.

'So that's why he was talking about my savings last night?' Ankush asked.

'Why are you trying so hard to look scandalized?'

Ankush's jaw stiffened. Then he spoke in a low, menacing voice: 'You think I don't know what he needs the money for? It's for the Bastard, isn't it? That child raper? And why

I'm having difficulty in looking scandalized? Because I'm confused. Because I can't fathom how you've lost all your sense of right and wrong.'

'I'm not asking you to pay for the Bastard. I'm asking you to lend some money to my father. He needs it.'

'It's the same thing, Taruna, the same thing.'

'So say no, it's okay,' Taruna said, her face twisted in anger.

Ankush exhaled through his mouth and looked outside his window. They were crossing Modipuram now. 'So that's what you discussed with them last night?' he said. When Taruna didn't answer, he assumed that the conversation was over, and convinced himself that Taruna was saying what she was because the stay at her parents' house had been strenuous for her. He allowed his mind to drift, and it went on its own inexplicable path.

After a while, he spoke about something altogether unrelated. 'Do you know you can boil live frogs in a vessel and they won't jump out of it?'

'What?' Taruna asked.

'Frogs, I'm talking about frogs. If you put them in cold water in a saucer and place it on a flame, the frogs won't jump out till they are boiled alive.'

'I don't know why you have to talk of this now.'

'Frogs can change their body temperature. So, as the water heats up, they keep adapting to the change in temperature by cooling off. They spend their energy on this cooling off. The water continues to heat up, of course, and the frogs continue to spend more and more energy. Eventually, when the water starts boiling, and the frogs have no more energy left, they start to, well, they start to feel the heat.'

'Why did you think of this?'

'Just because. My mind was just rambling.'

'Why did you think of this now?' Taruna's voice had an urgency to it.

'It means nothing, my love.'

'Am I a frog in boiling water?'

'Pfft.'

'Don't give me your smartness now, Ankush. What did you want to say? Is my father a frog in boiling water?'

'I didn't mean that.'

'Of course you didn't mean that.'

A longer silence reigned in the car this time, broken eventually after an hour by the driver. They were close to Meerut, and the driver suggested that they have lunch.

The Indigo turned into a place called Midway Motel. There were two air-conditioned buses parked in the large open space in front of the main food court. The buses had come from Dehradun and were headed towards Delhi. The drivers had made a lunch stop here for the passengers. Between the parking lot and the main food court was a separate shed for the drivers, where meals were served for hundred rupees. Ankush gave their driver the money.

Inside the food court, Ankush and Taruna sat at a corner table and soon got two plain dosas.

'We've let the situation get to us,' Ankush said to Taruna as he took a bite. 'We should stop fighting.'

'You say really nasty things sometimes, Ankush.'

'Look, I don't want to pay for that man,' Ankush said. Then, after a pause: 'I almost killed him last night, you know?'

Taruna looked at him, perplexed.

'I went to the other room when everyone was sleeping,' Ankush continued. 'I thought I should choke him with a cushion. Then I got scared that Ravi would wake up. I swear, I was close to doing it.'

'Should have tried it,' Taruna said coldly. 'I don't think Ravi would have stopped you.'

To Ankush, Taruna's even tone suggested that she did not believe him. He had thought that mentioning the incident from last night would make her see how he hated the Bastard as much as she did. He had hoped that their fight would end; that Taruna would see his side of things, especially his love for her. But she gave him no credence, and this made him angry. 'I won't pay for him,' he reiterated.

'Just for the record, Ankush, you were *not* asked to pay for *him*. You were asked to *lend money* to my father.'

'Which he intends to use for cleaning the old man's buttocks.'

Hearing this, Taruna's mind approached the logic that had lain in her head for a long time. Earlier, out of a need to believe in Ankush, she had refused it even to herself. But in this moment, she couldn't hold back. 'Has it ever occurred to you, Ankush,' she said, 'that this might be money that you *owe* my father?'

'That's silly,' Ankush said, looking at her with wide eyes.

'It's true that my father overspent in the wedding. But a significant portion was spent on the baraat's reception.'

'I know the line that you are going to take. I have thought ...'

'Would you call a baraat size of 250 a conservative number? In a city like Delhi?'

'Hey ...'

'Did you or your mother ever – and I mean, *ever* – offer to contribute anything to the expenses that my father bore? Which he bore so that *your guests* would feel that they had come to a grand wedding?'

'Taruna, I have thought of this. Trust me, had your father asked me, I would have contributed.'

'But why didn't it occur to you to offer it by yourself?'

'Because …' Ankush spread his arms in protest. 'Because that's convention. Because that's how it works, normally.'

'You are so comfortable with convention, right? My father is also following *convention* in providing for his own father.'

'But,' Ankush said, his voice sibilant, 'but we know what the Bastard did to you.'

'You sure that's not an excuse, Ankush? Because somehow I don't believe you. You felt that my father should have paid for the honeymoon. You didn't offer to pay for the wedding expenses. Now you're just refusing to lend money to him. There is a pattern. You sure you're not just a money-minded dude who mixes convention and convenience?'

'Bravo,' Ankush said loudly. 'What. A. Family! What a fucking, complicated family!'

People from other tables looked at theirs.

'You can say no, Ankush, and you have said no,' Taruna hissed. 'But don't try to prove how outrageous it is for me to ask you to help my father. I decide what is right and wrong here.'

'Oh really! And why are you the special one?'

'Because I am the one who was raped. And, please, don't try to clarify the situation to me. It can't be clearer to you than it is to me.'

'So you've forgiven him?'

'No, Ankush. And you know you're just asking that to further the argument.'

'Let me tell you something in plain terms,' Ankush said. 'It's not only you who decides what is right and wrong. Because you've made other people suffer with you. You've made your *parents* suffer for years. You've made *me* suffer. You know how dysfunctional you've been the whole week? And tell me if I haven't been my nicest. I tried my best to cheer you up while you kept reliving the shit that happened to you some twenty years back. You know what, I don't even trust you to stop thinking of him after he dies.'

Taruna sighed, looking down at the table. When she looked up, her eyes were wet. 'Let's not talk about this. It's alright, I don't blame you for refusing the money.'

But Ankush wasn't ready to take the invitation to let things pass. 'It's a scar. And you've grown up with it. But there are so many children in the world, you know, who have sexual experiences.'

'Are you really saying this? What are you saying?'

'That most people get better.'

The suggestion that she hadn't tried enough: Taruna had heard this all her life. 'Sometimes I think I don't know you, Ankush. You've no idea about sexual abuse but you theorize about it. Pass your wisdom about. You know what you sound like? Some kind of know-it-all dude who just sits around and explains things!'

A black rage clouded Ankush's eyes. He wanted nothing more in that moment than to hurt Taruna. 'Everyone has a childhood story, Taruna,' he said, 'yours just had an old man in it.'

'What?' Taruna gasped. Her eyes seemed to turn into stone. 'What did you just fucking say?'

'When I was fourteen, I fucked my neighbour. She was ten.'

Taruna clenched her jaws.

'And, you know, I still think of that sometimes and masturbate.'

She tried to slap him, but he managed to avoid it, catching her hand. 'Now what does that make me? A child raper?' he said.

'You ...' Taruna got up from her seat. There were tears were streaming down her cheeks.

'Where are you going?' Ankush asked.

She picked up the tissue paper from the table and wiped her eyes. 'To the toilet,' she said. 'Can I go to the toilet?'

Ankush let go of her hand, and watched her run towards the far corner of the food court. In the next two or three minutes, his rage subsided and he saw immediately how stupid he had just been. He had lied, just to be nasty; and he had been nastier than he had ever been. He saw that he didn't care about the money, that he would transfer the money to Taruna's father's account that afternoon itself. He didn't even care if he ever got it back. He pulled his hair in frustration, realizing that all he wanted now was to hold Taruna in his arms. He dialled her mobile number, but she cut the call. Then he called her again, after a couple of minutes. This time, the phone was switched off. He got up from the table and moved towards the toilets. He stood outside the ladies' toilet for a good ten minutes, but his wife didn't come out. He then noticed a passageway next to the toilet, and that it led outside the building. Perhaps Taruna had gone out for a walk. He decided to wait for another five minutes outside the ladies' toilet, but didn't have the patience. He hurriedly walked out of the passage, out in the open, and found himself out next to a bush. The highway was right in front of him. To his right was the front of the Midway Hotel, and he could see their driver standing beside the Indigo.

He walked up to the vehicle and asked the driver if he had seen Taruna. He hadn't. Ankush then saw the packed photograph on the front seat and for some reason remembered the picture in it: them standing close to a pillar, their faces approaching for a kiss.

There was a ringing on his phone. It was Taruna's mother.

'Beta, we have been trying Taruna's number for the last five minutes. Have you reached?'

'No, we are at a restaurant,' Ankush said. 'She's using the toilet.'

'Tell her that it's over,' Taruna's mother said.

'What?'

'He died half an hour ago. Tell Taruna. I think she'll be happy.'

Ankush didn't know what to say.

'Tell her that we are happy; that she should be happy too,' she said. Ankush heard her sniffle, and then there was nothing for him to do except cut the call.

He had to find his wife. He gasped for breath, looked around, ran. Taruna was nowhere to be seen. He had lost her. Then he noticed that one of the two Delhi-bound buses had left. He ran to the Indigo and asked the driver to drive towards Delhi. To catch the AC bus. The driver smiled at him in amusement.

# *The Mechanics of Silence*

Anjana thinks about the silent movie she has just finished watching.

The actors over-animated thanks to necessity.

The dialogues mimed, *shown*.

And they must be precise.

This constraint, Anjana thinks, this constraint of not being able to give sound and words to what is to be conveyed, must have made silent movie writers *creative*.

Creativity is from constraints – she feels like noting this down somewhere.

Creativity emerges from the ardour to work beyond one's constraints, she corrects herself.

Creativity is tunnelling through the constraints.

Creativity is going beyond a boundary, any boundary.

Even if that boundary is arbitrary and self-made.

So why doesn't she call him?

---

Everyone in the silent movie is dead now.

That brute of a hero, his gestures brimming with strength, is dead.

That radiant heroine, a jailer to the camera's gaze, is dead.

The director is dead.

Everyone who ever had to do anything with the movie is dead.

She plays the movie again.

The movie is now a pageant of death.

She feels as if she is ogling at the actions and gestures (even if make-believe) of the dead.

The movements of the actors acquire a new meaning now.

The certainty of their death weighs down upon everything.

All comedy is now a larger human tragedy.

The overacting doesn't look like overacting now.

It looks like lived life.

The movie is a ruin in perfect condition, she thinks.

It is its own contradiction.

She needs to distract herself.

Maybe silent cinema should be a genre today, she thinks, just so that writers have an entirely different creative outlet.

Should she call him?

---

Her throat feels dry.

She shuts her laptop and goes to the kitchen.

She drinks a lot of water.

There is still thirst.

She keeps the bottle inside the fridge and goes to the bathroom to look at the mirror there.

Her face is her face.

He will not call.

She thinks of touching herself.

No.

She should go outdoors.

She should stop doing random things like watching silent movies on a Saturday.

She should run on Saturday mornings.

She is getting fat.

She washes her face and pins up her hair.

For a second, she appears beautiful to herself.

She puts on some shoes and steps outside the apartment.

On the street, the spring sun, clear and liquid, goes through her.

She reminds herself to stay away from cigarettes the whole day.

Some of the silent movie directors must have known that the silence of movies was temporary; that one day movies won't be silent any more.

A camera could track her right now.

Right now, a camera tracking her would convey that she is going somewhere.

But she is not going anywhere in particular.

Where should she go?

*The silence of silent movies is a felix culpa that allows us to know sound and soundlessness intimately.*

She could go right or left.

Inside the mall, there is a strain of classical music – Western classical music.

Anjana thinks of Schubert's *Impromptus*.

He could play a couple of them, though not very well.

She doesn't know where to go inside the mall; some of the stores haven't even opened yet.

Not that she is here to visit the stores that are still closed.

Or have just opened.

This coming-to-the-mall with nothing to do is not happening for the first time.

She wonders if it is a signifier of some malaise in her.

Like previous instances of being purposeless in the mall, she starts moving towards the top floor, where the food court is.

There is a series of escalators to be taken.

She has always found the appellation *food court* bemusing.

She has always found the serrated steps of escalators dangerous.

She reaches the food court.

There are people there.

Are these people like her, lonely folks who come to food courts inside malls?

She goes to McDonald's and orders a meal.

She nibbles at the burger and fries, but is not really interested in eating.

The camera could be in front of her, focused on her eyes.

The movie will be a silent one.

She will not look directly into the camera.

But the gaze of the camera will make her confront the malaise.

She will probably cry.

The televisions of the food court flicker to life together.

They are telecasting a live cricket match.

India is playing.

He must be watching.

She watches.

She is thankful that there is something she can watch.

It seems that India is in a tight spot, but it also seems that India will win.

She munches the burger a little more.

The food court begins to fill with more people.

Couples and families are joining in now; the singletons are becoming a minority.

The din in the place is increasing.

She listens carefully to the increments in sound.

There is that rustle at the food counters.

There are shout-outs to family members, things said loudly, loud laughter.

Kids.

She decides to gape at the action at a distant table, distant enough for its sounds not to reach her.

The kid is engrossed in the fries.

The father looks up at the television while dipping his burger in ketchup.

The mother has a bad posture while eating, and just stares at the food trays in front of her.

What would a silent movie director make of this scene?

The actors aren't animated enough; so something will have to give.

The camera can move.

The camera will slowly move towards them.

The movement may mean picking out this Indian family as *the* Indian family.

The camera should keep going closer.

There should be silence, unforced, unexamined.

The camera should eventually position the audience right behind the father's head and trace his gaze, towards the television.

The camera should then zoom in on the television, but it should show the action on the screen only as a blur.

What will this scene convey?

As far as *the* Indian family is concerned, nothing.

Or perhaps the camera shouldn't move.

It should stay where Anjana is, and keep gaping.

Some unsayable is bared when a gaze fixates on something with life.

But there should be silence.

There is a loud roar in the food court now.

The elements of this roar are indiscernible.

The roar just is.

It is a roar that enmeshes appetites, desires, grouses, anger, discomfort.

In that, this roar is akin to silence.

But roars and silences, both need subjects; they both need to belong to someone or something for them to convey anything.

This roar at the food court belongs to the crowd here.

The silence of their relationship belongs to __________.

Why are things so difficult to end?

---

Anjana is done with the burger and the fries and the soft drink.

She just sits there, watching India's advance in the cricket match.

India will win.

He is watching.

He will be happy if India wins.

The roar at the food court is a kind of silence – she convinces herself of this.

The food court – the mall – is a festival of ... what ... life?

If it is a *something* of life, that something is not a festival.

The food court – the mall – is a depression of life, a trough.

She is being insane.

Becoming insane.

She feels bad that she buys a lot of groceries and yet eats from McDonald's.

The silent movie she watched today, *The Docks of New York*, was released in 1928.

Should she buy something?

She gets up from the seat and shoves the tray's refuse down a bin's rectangular mouth.

She puts the tray on top of the bin.

She looks at the television.

India is very close to winning.

The roar is still there, unwavering, unperturbed.

A good-looking man passes by, holding a McDonald's tray.

Anjana feels like telling him: 'Don't eat that garbage; come home and I'll fix you some vegetables.'

The roar is there, unremitting, loud, silent.

She moves toward the escalators.

She will now go down down down.

Then she will walk back home.

It is likely, she knows, that she will watch another silent movie.

Instead of showing dialogue as text, could silent movies just show *any* text instead?

She gets new ideas when she watches silent movies.

It is good to have new ideas.

Silent movie characters can then be truly silent; they don't have to say a thing.

Is there a movie like that?

---

The afternoon is hot.

Anjana wants to put something inside her vagina.

She fixes herself a drink, a sort of rum punch.

She googles for the best silent movies ever.

'I'm a woman,' she speaks aloud, for no reason at all.

The grill outside her window casts a grilly shadow on her ceiling.

I am decent, she thinks.

In the world of silent movies, there can be no wastage of words; the displayed text has to serve a great purpose.

She feels like buying a video camera online.

She feels like making a silent movie.

# *Compassionate Grounds*

The news registered a whole minute after she cut the call. She was still in the party dress that she'd been too drunk to change from a few hours ago. To start, she stumbled to the toilet and brushed her teeth, hoping that it would conclusively wake her up and mitigate the alcohol smell in her mouth. She then removed the dress, breaking one of its straps while doing so. The kurta she put on was cut in the low, round-neck fashion, and the salwar was a patiala. Finding the whole ensemble improper, she changed it and wore a duller combination instead. She stuffed her clothes into one of Mahesh's suitcases, careful not to disturb him too much with the opening and shutting of the wardrobes. Right after zipping the bag, she realized that she hadn't put the toothbrush in. She spent some time looking for it, finally finding it on her bedside table. Seconds after stuffing in the toothbrush, she opened the suitcase again, this time to put in a pair of slippers. Then she paced around the apartment, not knowing why, her mind buzzing like late-night radio. She opened her wardrobe again and donned an old, cream-coloured cardigan, finding it somehow most appropriate. She remembered tampons and put some in the suitcase. After giving a thought to the number of days she might have to stay in Muzaffarnagar – at least two weeks, she guessed – she opened the suitcase again to count the number of undergarments she had packed. She tried to make a list of other essentials in her mind, but her brain was incapable of this kind of meticulousness. A headache felt as if it was a spear pushing deep in her head. She looked around for her phone. She had affixed it to the charger after the party ended; so it had full battery. Or was it Mahesh who had done that? She thumbed it open and sat on the bed and checked Facebook on impulse. There were photos of last night's party and she had been tagged in some. She removed the tags. There were more photos in a WhatsApp group. Jerks, she thought, and, resolving not to pose with Mahesh's friends ever again, switched the display off.

She left the apartment, slowly clicking the main door shut. In the lift, she closed her eyes and fell into an instant sleep, such that the tinkle of the elevator's arrival at the basement felt too loud to her. In the parking lot, ten steps away from the space allotted to Mahesh's cars, the fatigue suddenly overcame her. She collapsed. She was somehow aware of what was happening, but felt powerless before it.

She woke up some minutes later, with the realization that she was too tired and hungover to leave right away. So she decided to go back and rest a bit more, perhaps for an hour or so.

She got back in the lift and got off at the fourth floor. She then rang the bell to their apartment. Mahesh took a full five minutes to open the door, and could only manage a blank look of incomprehension. To be fair, it would be a mild shock for anyone: the woman who should have been in his bed was standing outside his door, with a suitcase.

'What ... were you trying to leave me, Gunjan?' he said.

'No,' Gunjan said, pulling the suitcase past him and into the bedroom.

'Then what?' he said and followed her into the bedroom.

Mahesh had only his shorts on. Gunjan noticed that, unlike her, he had managed to remove his party wear before sleeping. She crashed on their bed with her back towards him, crushing her face against a soft pillow. 'My father … he passed away,' she said.

'Oh.'

The *oh* was one of relief, not shock or empathy. She turned to face him.

'Then … you should go,' he said. 'Right?'

Gunjan sighed and let her head fall on the pillow again. She would remember this *oh* from Mahesh. She would remember how he didn't have the right words. But she was feeling only a minor anger towards him. Had she been sad, it would have hurt her more. But somehow she wasn't sad. She closed her eyes.

'Tell me what happened, sweetheart?' she heard Mahesh say in a soft voice. He was sitting next to her now, running his hand over her head. He was like a child in moments like this one, when he sensed he had done something wrong.

⁂

It was the first day of January and Gunjan's father had died. Nine days ago, on 23 December, her grandfather had died. The old man had passed away in his sleep and now her father had passed away minutes after waking up. On the morning of the first day of a new year. At around 6 a.m. She had talked to him on the phone last night, before Mahesh's friends had starting streaming in for the New Year's Eve party at their apartment. It was a brief conversation, in which he had stressed how important it was for her to be present in

Muzaffarnagar on 4 January – the day of her grandfather's terahvi. He had arranged a big lunch and invited hundreds of people. 'It's an important day,' he had said.

And now he was dead.

Mahesh woke her up three hours later. He told her that there had been repeated rings on her phone and that he had had to pick up the last one. 'It was your bua,' he said, 'asking how long it would take you.'

Gunjan didn't like that Mahesh had picked up the phone. She complained about not being woken up earlier and left the house within the next ten minutes, after having the cup of coffee he had prepared for her. She took the black Jetta, the least showy of Mahesh's four cars. In her first attempt in the morning, she had unthinkingly picked up the keys of the black Merc that she had been driving the past few days. That would have been something for Muzaffarnagar!

It being the first day of January, there were not many cars on Delhi's roads, and Gunjan drove through the city without much difficulty. At one of the signals, she dialled her mother's number. It was picked up by Chhoti Maami. 'I'm on my way, Maami. I will reach by one.' Not wanting to hear a response from the other side, she cut the call immediately.

She recalled the phone call the night her grandfather had passed away. Her father's message had been terse, his voice matter-of-fact. He had to be like that: grandfather's condition had deteriorated irrecoverably at the onset of winter and everyone in the family knew he wouldn't survive the season. The news hadn't bothered her at all. She remembered going out for dinner with Mahesh that day, then watching a movie at home, also having sex. The next morning, she had thought about going to Muzaffarnagar; but then she ended up making a work-related excuse to her father, whose only demand was that she be present on the terahvi day.

She encountered a dense fog once she crossed Ghaziabad. She had to slow the car down, and the added concentration she had to put into driving made her headache worse. What a fucked-up morning, she thought, then felt guilty about thinking like that.

She and Mahesh had partied hard last night. It was the second time they had celebrated the coming of the new year together, their relationship being eighteen months old. Her mind went to their first meeting at a bookstore in McLeod Ganj where, over coffee and books, she had noticed Mahesh's salt and pepper hair, his calm attention to books, his strong forearms, and several obscure hints of what she would only discover later – old money. From their flirtations, Gunjan found out that he had been *backpacking* in the most expensive hotel in McLeod Ganj – an irony to which he was insulated by his wealth. He invited her there for the evening and Gunjan accepted without a second thought. The hotel was a vintage property with a dozen or more suites, with generous balconies adding a shade of regality to the views offered. It was partly Mahesh's balcony that seduced Gunjan that evening.

At thirty-seven then, Mahesh was eleven years her senior. After they got together, this age difference became a hindrance for Gunjan's friends. One by one, they ceased being in contact with her. But she didn't care. For a long enough period in the first year of their relationship, she had even suspected that she loved Mahesh. He was somewhat naive, but only in the way a *nice* rich person ought to be. Things were easy for him, and he had the basic sense to not make them artificially difficult. As a prospects-shorn advertising professional who did creative work but could never aspire to a more-than-decent salary, she felt inclined to enjoy her partner's money. For her self-esteem, it was enough that Mahesh never treated her like something that he had won, though she had known right from their early days that some of his friends held that view.

They had met in late May 2013 and by September she had moved into Mahesh's flat in Vasant Vihar. He, in fact, owned the entire building, which housed eight large flats in it. The other seven flats had been rented out to expatriate families. These were people from France, Germany, or the Scandinavian countries. Gunjan was friendly with all of them, even the kids; none of the white people ever made her feel awkward. At get-togethers on the terrace, the men sometimes tried to put a casual hand on her shoulder, or even around her waist, but their gestures always lacked the proprietorial air of Mahesh's Indian friends.

Gunjan and Mahesh seldom discussed the issue of love with each other. He had never been married. She thanked her luck for that, for there was no way she could have dealt with a more complex scenario. But she knew that Mahesh had strong feelings for her, and that he would, at some point, raise the question of marriage. On her side, there was no possibility of a lifelong commitment. Once she had even tried to make that clear to Mahesh. 'I don't come from a place where a woman can marry an older man,' she had said. But Mahesh had dismissed it with a smile. As for the status quo, she wanted it unchanged as long as she could help it. Mahesh was good in bed, good in hygiene, good in manners, and he was rich.

She took the Meerut bypass and the Delhi FM station, which had remained switched on from the beginning, suffered a bout of static that brought her attention to it. It struck her that it was probably wrong to play music. She blamed herself for not thinking of it earlier and switched off the radio. The fog had lessened considerably by now. To reduce the sudden emptiness she felt inside the car, she rolled down the windows – a cold wind gushed in with a pleasing sound. She tried to call forth some snippets of her life involving her father, to remember him, but nothing specific came to her except the three words that had inexplicably stuck to her mind ever since she had received the news: *a simple man*. A simple man, made to live and die in Muzaffarnagar. He had provided for her for the majority of her life. And she had needed him many times even after she had started earning in Delhi – after she had become *independent* – to help set up a monthly deposit in a mutual fund, to help move her meagre furniture whenever she changed apartments, to pay for a trip to Sri Lanka that all her friends could somehow afford and she couldn't, to help file a police complaint against a guy who had been stalking her online, and so on. Her father had travelled from Muzaffarnagar to Delhi on each occasion of her need, except the times when she had asked him not to. Lately, since the time she had started with Mahesh, she hadn't needed to fall back on him.

*A simple man*. He died without ever using WhatsApp or Facebook, Gunjan thought. The highway cleaved the fields between Meerut and Khatauli, and as her Jetta paced through the equidistant shadows of eucalyptus trees (the sun was out now), she wondered if there was some great insight hidden in that fact. It hit her then that she only understood her father as a certain *type* of man; that she didn't know much about the individual that she would soon be required to mourn.

It was two in the afternoon when she entered the main gate of the Sugarcane Research Station, the government-run facility where her father had worked as a senior plant pathologist. The facility had the obvious aim of improving cane yields in the highly fertile zone of western U.P. The research on new cane breeds or pathologies was carried out in the hectares of government-owned farms that constituted a majority of the acreage in the Muzaffarnagar facility. Owing to this, the whole place was often simply called 'ganna farm' or, even more simply, 'farm'. Gunjan had spent most of her growing-up years in the residential colony inside the farm. After his last promotion three years ago, her father had been given a flat-roofed bungalow here.

Outside the bungalow now were a dozen or more cars parked on either side of the road. A driveway descended from the road and ran for fifteen or so metres before being halted by a small portico-like space. Next to the driveway, running along the length of the house, was a kitchen garden. There were groups of men standing all along the driveway. Finding no other place to park the Jetta, Gunjan honked once to signal that she wanted to park the car there. It was only when she rolled down the windows and there was a hush of recognition from the crowd that she was given the space to manoeuvre her vehicle. Most people trampled the radish in the garden. Gunjan knew it had been planted by her father.

She got out of the car and opened the trunk. It was empty! She had forgotten to bring the suitcase. She must have taken it to the apartment after collapsing in the basement and then forgotten to take it during her second departure.

Her younger maama ran up to her. He hugged her and began sobbing. She found herself patting his back, as if consoling him. She could feel how his chest heaved. 'I forgot my suitcase,' she said.

'Come inside, beta, come inside. Your mother is …'

They walked towards the house. Gunjan felt stupid and angry for forgetting the suitcase. Then she saw from close the damage that the crowd was doing to her father's radish crop and it made her angrier. She could recognize most men as relatives and acquaintances. 'Please, you people get off the garden,' she yelled at everybody. 'Get off it. Come inside or stand on the road, not in the garden.' The area was emptied in seconds, even before she had entered the house.

Inside the big living room, her mother was seated on a central sofa, surrounded by women. Seeing Gunjan, she began crying loudly. Gunjan rushed to her and embraced her. Her bua, her father's only sister, embraced them both. They stayed in that position for some time, till Gunjan felt her mother whispering something in her ear. She strained to listen. 'Ask Chhoti Maami … she is in the kitchen … ask her to give you something to eat,' her mother was saying.

What kind of a creature is a parent? Gunjan thought. She was hungry, and her mother knew that she was hungry. Even now.

She broke the hug, stood up and walked towards the kitchen. There were people everywhere in the house, and somehow for her this meant that she couldn't cry even if she wanted to. 'Cry, beta … it helps,' someone said.

Maami gave her chapattis with curried potatoes. She was quite functional, Gunjan noticed. 'The food is from the neighbours – the Sharmas,' Maami said, pointing in the general direction of the neighbouring bungalow. 'It was Mr Sharma who rushed Bhaisaab to the hospital this morning.' She paused after saying this, as if allowing Gunjan a second in which to feel a tug of gratitude towards the man. 'It's not shubh to cook in this kitchen till the cremation,' she continued, 'but in case you want more chapattis, just tell me quietly. The women won't notice.' Gunjan nodded, not knowing how else to respond. She took the plate to the innermost room, where there was no one. There, she exhaled as if for the first time. How would she manage without her suitcase? After a while, Maami came in to ask if she wanted another chapatti. 'Where's Papa?' Gunjan asked instead.

'In the bathroom,' Maami answered. 'The big one. They brought in ice slabs just before you came. It probably wasn't necessary … It's winter, na … but they put the body on it nevertheless. He was in this room earlier.'

'Where did he … pass away? How?'

'Your mother and bua were sleeping in the main bedroom,' Maami said, referring to the room adjacent to the living room. 'Your father was sleeping on the living room dewan. He woke up around five in the morning, vomited. Didi said he was complaining of acidity. She gave him some cold milk. Then, an hour later, she found him … still.'

'Hmm.'

'His teeth were clenched. His pyjama … his pyjama was wet.'

'What?' Gunjan shook her head in incomprehension.

'Your Maama said it means it was the heart … and that it wasn't sudden. He felt pain. Probably felt helpless for a few minutes.'

Maami lingered for a moment before exiting the room. Not knowing how to react, Gunjan found herself nodding. When she brought the next morsel to her mouth, her hand was shaking. Was she supposed to have a look at the body now?

The toilet-cum-bathroom had been used exclusively by her grandfather when he was alive. For the old man's comfort, her father had had it fitted with a Western-style pot. There was a steel handlebar affixed to the wall next to the toilet pot, to help in sitting and standing up. On the other side, a thin, two-feet high wall separated the toilet area from the bath area. Her father now lay on thick slabs of ice in this latter area – next to where his father shat for the last few years of his life. He was covered with a white sheet, and for a moment Gunjan was curious about whether he was naked under it. She took half a step forward and looked at his face. It was as if it had been pulled up from his forehead. His mouth was partly open, and it seemed that the life of him had escaped from right there.

She stepped out. There were four–five women – her mother's cousins – seated in the adjacent bedroom. They looked at her with sad eyes, expecting her to cry. One of them goaded her to cry. But Gunjan just moved to the verandah outside, and from there to the open, walled area that could be called a backyard.

She saw her father's scooter parked there, and next to it her old bicycle. The cycle had been repaired, and it surprised her to see it in a good state. She sat on the cycle, moved its pedals backwards to make that pleasant whirring sound. She remembered how her father had taught her how to ride when she was a child. He had held the carrier for her, run after her, had never let her fall. But when she had become an expert, he had not allowed her to take the cycle to school for a few years. He had relented only after tenth standard, when it became impossible for him to ferry her to and from the school and the many tuitions.

She got off the cycle and went to the verandah, somewhat content with having had a memory of her father. In the living room, her mother was still surrounded by people consoling her. She wasn't crying now. But she was still repeating 'why did you go so soon?' in a soft murmur. Gunjan went outside, among the men. No one had dared to step into the kitchen garden. She approached Bade Maama and asked, 'When is the cremation?'

'We will take him in another ten–fifteen minutes.'

'Only men are allowed, right?' she asked.

'Yes, usually. You have to be by your mother's side when we take him. You have to console each other.'

Bade Maama had always comported himself as a stern person, with a liking for protocol and its adherence. He would be the last person to note any lack of grief on her face: for him, life was one situation after another, all to be processed.

She did namaste to the men she recognized. Her father's three brothers were here, and Jagvir Chacha, the youngest among them, had tears in his eyes. The eldest one, Tauji, was smoking a cigarette. He had had his heart operated a couple of years ago and was prohibited from smoking. She had never been close enough to him, so as to be able to approach him and demand for the cigarette to be stubbed. The urge she had to suppress was a different one – to ask him for a couple of puffs herself. Jagvir Chacha walked up to her and hugged her, crying profusely on her shoulder. The other two also approached them and patted her head affectionately. Nothing brought tears to her eyes. 'Go inside, beta,' Tauji said. 'Take care of your mother.'

Gunjan sat on the sofa, next to her mother, looking down at the cracked granite floor. No matter how old she was, she would always be a child in this house. No matter the exigency, her lunch would be a priority. Tauji had just asked her to take care of her mother, and although he had meant for Gunjan to be by her mother's side when her father's body was being taken for the cremation, she wondered if his words portended a fundamental change. No one had ever asked Gunjan to take care of anybody.

Her mother was next to her, exhausted from all the crying. Gunjan wondered what was going through her mind, and it occurred to her that it might not be all about the past: it was possible that her mother was less saddened by the loss of a husband and more terrified by the questions of her own future. Despite almost three decades of service, her father had not been able to buy or build a house of his own. 'It'll be alright, Mummy; it'll be alright,' Gunjan felt compelled to say. Her mother looked at her and gave a feeble smile.

Just then the cell phone in Gunjan's kameez pocket began to ring. It was Mahesh. She felt it inappropriate to talk to him at this moment and cut the call. Then she asked her mother, 'Papa was using my cycle?'

'Yes. He had begun to like the exercise.'

They shared a glance for they both realized the futility of the last word, exercise. To Gunjan, it seemed unfair that a man who had begun cycling again had to die of a heart failure.

When the body was lifted for the cremation, Gunjan's mother wailed. A tense calm was restored only after the group of men left. But the news of the death was still travelling, and each time a new relative turned up at the door, she would start crying again.

After a while, Gunjan found the space to make a call to Mahesh.

'Hello.'

'Hello. How are you?'

'I forgot my suitcase.'

'Yes, you did. How are you going to manage?'

'I'll buy stuff, I guess.'

'So … how are things?'

'Hmm … difficult.'

'Yeah. Your mother?'

'She just cries.'

'Hmm …'

'You know, my father was using a cycle to go to work.'

'Hmm …'

'Well, guess we should talk later. Bye?'

'Bye. Take care.'

❧

At dusk, only some close family members remained in the house. This included her mother's two brothers and their wives, her bua, and Jagvir Chacha. The other two paternal uncles had left.

Gunjan learnt that a pundit had already been consulted and it had been decided that her father's terahvi would also happen on the fourth of January, along with her grandfather's. The reasons behind this decision were unknown to Gunjan, but she welcomed it nevertheless, for it meant that formal mourning would not exceed three days. Several times through the evening, Gunjan heard one or another family member moan about 'god's strange ways', or about the 'intense love between father and son', or how 'Ranbir-ji was called to heaven by his father', and so on. She did not resonate with any of these emotions, for she believed that even if an almighty god existed, he or she could not possibly care about these things. That her grandfather and father had died inside ten days of each other was just harsh coincidence.

A similar set of people had assembled the previous week as well, when her grandfather had died. Her bua had decided, not very unhappily, to stay back till the terahvi. Gunjan presumed there wasn't this much sadness in the air then. Her father and her uncles would have struck light conversations. Had she been present, they would have asked her about her life in Delhi, and would have advised her to make peace with the idea of marriage, and so on. She knew from her mother that they had even opened a bottle late in the night. Her father had gotten his eyes moist a couple of times. Her uncles had responded each time by refilling his glass.

Her mother was in charge of the kitchen then. Now, with her being incapacitated by grief, the two maamis were managing the cooking. Around dinner time, there was an electricity cut. Everyone, save her mother, assembled in the living room. Gunjan realized that her mother was alone in the main bedroom and, as if goaded on by the darkness, she went there. Finding her mother on the bed, she lay next to her.

'How are you, Mummy?' she whispered.

'I'm okay.'

She touched her mother's forehead and swept back the hair that had fallen on her face.

'You haven't shed a tear, my child,' her mother said.

Gunjan didn't know the right response to that. She had been dreading this being pointed out by her.

'Your father was a good man.'

'Yes, Mummy.'

'His brothers always took advantage of him. But he remained good to them till the end.'

'Yes.'

'He loved you very much.'

'Yes, Mummy.'

'He was never very open to us. That was his nature. It was tough to know what was on his mind. But last week, he was quite unhappy.'

'Why? He missed Dadaji?'

'No … not only that.'

'Did he say anything?'

'Some things. To me. To your bua. It all seems so strange now.'

'What?'

'That our children don't want to know us.'

'Is that what he said?'

'Yes. I think he wished that you had been here after your grandfather passed away. I told him that he should talk to you more often.'

'He did call me yesterday' Gunjan said. 'He wished me a Happy New Year.'

---

The next day, relatives from farther away visited the house. Her mother wasn't crying all the time and her maamis were serving tea to anyone who didn't refuse it altogether. The men were out ensuring supplies for the ceremony on the fourth; they needed to follow up with shocked shopkeepers with whom her father had already placed orders. Bade Maama's car was used for any trip to the city. Just before lunch, when the men were out, Gunjan took the Jetta to the market to buy substitutes for all that she had left behind in the suitcase in Delhi. Hers was the biggest car in the tiny market, a cause for jams. She bought some plain T-shirts, track pants, slacks, undergarments, a pair of slippers, and some sanitary pads. Her reasoning was that it would be fine to just hide the T-shirts under a jacket or under one of her mother's cardigans. As she was driving back from the crowded Shiv Chowk, a scooter bumped into the Jetta. She rolled down the window and yelled at the scooterist, but he just grinned back at her, mightily amused.

Once outside the house, she examined the resulting scratch on the car – it ran the entire length of the right-side rear door. She shook her head and walked inside. Apart from the family members, there were three or four visitors in the living room; she nodded to everyone and walked past.

In the innermost room, she found Chhoti Maami hunched over a steaming cup of tea. Gunjan gestured to her to keep quiet and dialled her boss in the ad agency to inform him that she would not be coming to work any time soon. This was difficult, because she had used her grandfather's death as an excuse to skip work for the whole of the previous week. When the boss asked for the reason now, she had to tell the truth about her father's death. He sounded unconvinced, but did not commit the indecency of displaying his incredulity on the phone. 'Okay, take care' is what he cut the call with.

'You didn't go to work the previous week?' Maami asked Gunjan once the call was over. She was smiling. 'Hope you had fun.'

Gunjan smiled back. Maami was in her mid-thirties; an attractive woman. Of a fit age to marry Mahesh – the stray thought entered Gunjan's mind. Maami taught biology in a secondary school in Noida, where Chhote Maama ran a pharma distribution company.

'Well, you couldn't have known,' Maami said before walking out of the room.

Gunjan then thought of WhatsApping Mahesh about the scratch on his car. She typed the message but didn't send it. She knew it wouldn't bother him one bit; and for a moment she felt angry that it was so – that Mahesh's money allowed him a calmness that could even be misconstrued as having spiritual origins. It was the very thing that had attracted her to him, she reminded herself.

⁂

On the morning of the fourth, Gunjan's mother and bua decided that it would be improper of her to wear T-shirt and track pants on the terahvi. They insisted that she try one of Chhoti Maami's saris. Given that Chhoti Maami and Gunjan were nearly the same size, the blouse fit satisfactorily. When Gunjan tried on the whole outfit, it was unanimously decided that she would be wearing it for the day.

The arrangements had all been made by her father. There was a large, open lawn in front of the farm director's bungalow. Her father had taken permission to set up a tent in the lawn, to seat guests there – all facing a picture of his own father. There would be a buffet lunch after the formal mourning, prepared by the halwai troupe that he had fixed. But now, his own framed picture accompanied his father's photograph, a sight that made people sigh and shake their heads uneasily.

Gunjan noticed how her grandfather's picture was in colour, and had clearly been photoshopped to improve his appearance. This was her father's attention to detail. But his own picture was a recent one, from one of his field trips, and in black-and-white print. The picture had been arranged in the morning, she knew, when it hit Jagvir Chacha that nobody had thought of it. He then went to a cyber cafe with a flash drive, but unfortunately the guy only had a black-and-white printer. If there was any positive from the photo, it was that it presented her father's death as some sort of afterthought, or rather as the simple shock that it veritably was. Nevertheless, Gunjan could not escape feeling responsible for the quality of the photo. She should have cared for such details, for what else was she doing anyway.

The apparent cosmic cruelty in the fact that her father's arrangements now provided for his own mourning, that his own portrait accompanied his father's in his public invitation for sadness, was commented on by several people during the day. Each time Gunjan heard this sentiment reflected even broadly, she felt irritated, the way one would be while reading a cliché in a magazine article. There was nothing more notable than sheer absurdity in her father passing away a few days after her grandfather. Each attempt to grant it a significance larger than just that was irrational, according to her. It was as if people could not accept the reality of these two deaths unless they could explain them as a single, tragic story, driven by an internal logic whose complex justness had to be accepted.

The day turned out to be rather hectic. Almost everyone who came to the terahvis in the tent also paid a visit to the house, which was only a hundred or so metres away. The kitchen garden was thoroughly trampled without any protest from Gunjan, though she wondered what would remain of the last of her father's *additions* to the world. Inside the house, any woman meeting her mother would invariably cry, and this astounded Gunjan each time it happened. How were these women so quick with tears? She herself hadn't cried even once. Even to make a forlorn face, she could summon only a general sadness implicit in life and nothing related to her father in specific.

She was, not surprisingly, the centre of attention among the women. She overheard many of them talking about her, about how good she looked (sari!), how she was in her late twenties and didn't have much time left, how her mother now surely needed help in finding the best match for her, and so on. Some of the women walked up to her and hugged her, often saying something that amounted to: *you have to take care of your mother now*. One of them asked her to pull the sari pallu over her head.

Outside the house, her uncles made her meet several men along the day, men their age or thereabouts. Many of these *uncles* recited a memory of her father's. A couple of them had made short speeches under the tent, where a mike-and-speaker system had been set up.

Then there were the kids. They ran to and from the sequestered narrow road connecting the house to the lawn, squealing with excitement about the number of games they could concoct in the open space. A game of rudimentary kabaddi was set up in one half of the kitchen garden. Every once a while, a father would try to hush a kid into understanding the gravity of the situation. The kid in question would nod understandingly, only to relapse into jollity a few minutes later.

By afternoon, the terahvi was more or less over. The families that had stayed back counted themselves as the close relatives, and had moved to occupy the chairs set up in the backyard. There were two rounds of tea, both prepared and offered by her maamis. Surprisingly for Gunjan, sadness seemed less and less pervasive. She caught light tones in conversations, people using the occasion to discuss their own lives. She was somewhat relieved to see the social function of such a gathering manifest itself.

It was only around six in the evening that the last of the relatives left. There was another round of tea then, for the family members who had been there since the beginning. Gunjan learnt that her maamas would leave the next day, in the morning, and so would her bua. Jagvir Chacha would stay back a couple of days to sort out the papers. Which papers, Gunjan wondered.

While sipping tea, her elder maama elaborated upon how everything – the tent, the food, the mike system, the flowers – had already been paid for by 'Bhaisaab' and started sobbing violently, something that was so out of line with his general demeanour that it shocked everyone. Gunjan's mother consoled him over several minutes. This burst of grief made Gunjan uncomfortable – she shared none of its intensity. She got up and went inside her room. She was actually somewhat ashamed of her ineptitude at being sad, and it didn't help knowing that everyone in the family had seen this numbness only as a sign of shock. There had been moments in the day when she had felt like a fraud, like she was someone impersonating her father's daughter, or like an actor caught inside a film she had never chosen to be a part of.

She changed out of the sari and put on more comfortable clothes, with an old sweater on top. It was building up to be a very cold night, and just as she considered switching on the room heater, the electricity went off. She thought of calling Mahesh, but abandoned the idea as she didn't have anything to say. With him, too, she had often felt like a fraud, as if the life they shared didn't belong to her. And what was that life? In the darkness of the room, the answer seemed easier. They partied, they went to plays and art exhibitions, met friends in the pubs of Hauz Khas or Gurgaon; she let him fuck her the way he wanted, even enjoyed it most of the time; he bought her Calvin Klein dresses, let her change the paintings in the apartment, let her change the furniture as well; she used one of his credit cards, drove his Merc to an office where her peers came on scooters; they had gone to the Philippines last year; she had met his mother twice …

And all this was lived by someone else, she thought, an avatar of hers that was committed to a din and clutching on to its garbled tunes. It weighed upon her that even as she felt out of her element here in Muzaffarnagar, in her late fathers' government-granted bungalow – with its chipped paint, its dimming tube lights, its power cuts, its bureaucratic squalor – Mahesh's swanky apartment in Delhi had never felt like much of a home either. But the real malaise, she knew, was that she was already jaded enough to regard this homelessness as definitive of adulthood.

The next morning, her maamas and maamis made to leave – something that brought fresh tears to her mother's eyes. Bade Maama spoke of Bhaisaab's kindness, and announced how he was what he was because of the twenty-thousand-rupee loan that Gunjan's father had given him twenty years ago. Chhote Maama repeated the dismay of the twin tragedy that had struck the family.

After the emotions, the uncles called Gunjan closer and told her that it was now her task to take care of her mother, that she should not give her mother any stress, and that in a year or maximum two years, she should get married. They then asked her to dedicate some time to sorting her father's papers.

'Find the insurance papers as soon as possible,' Chhote Maama said. 'The companies throw tantrums with late claims.'

She nodded.

'And Gunjan, there is one more thing,' said Bade Maama, before looking at Gunjan's mother hesitantly.

'Yes, tell her,' her mother said. 'Explain it to her and explain it to Jagvir too.' She then went inside to call Jagvir Chacha, who was in one of the rooms with Bua.

'The thing is,' Bade Maama continued, 'as you know, your father was a government servant. In U.P. government service. And, although we are all immeasurably saddened by his untimely death, there is some good in the timing. Given that it was god's will and was always going to happen.'

What Maama said was too cryptic for Gunjan. 'What do you mean? How is the timing fortunate?'

'You know your father was due to retire at the end of this month?' Chhote Maama said.

Gunjan felt shame at not having cared enough to remember. Of course the retirement was in January – she'd spoken to her father about this a couple of times last year. Is that why her father was disappointed with her when grandfather died? Had he sensed that she had forgotten? This bungalow would have needed to be vacated soon, and her parents would have taken a place on rent. Was that on her father's mind? The change that a move to a rented apartment would entail, how it would emphasize his failure to build a house for himself.

'Since he was still in employment at the time of his death,' Bade Maama said, 'his demise means that you have some options, as granted by the government.'

Jagvir Chacha came and stood next to Gunjan. He was five years younger than her father, but he had never been as physically active. He had a stoop and looked older, frailer. He could be next, Gunjan thought for a moment.

'What options?' Gunjan asked her maama.

'The department rule says that in the event of an employee's passing, a direct dependent can seek a job from the same government department. On compassionate grounds.'

'Okay,' said Gunjan.

'Had Bhaisaab passed away post retirement,' Chhote Maama said, 'say, after a month, this option would not have existed.'

'That's why I said that there was some good in the timing,' Bade Maama said. 'It's as if Bhaisaab thought of giving back to his family even in his time of death.'

'Bhabhiji can easily take the option,' Jagvir Chacha joined the conversation.

'It is likely to be something clerical; something you can easily manage,' Bade Maama said to his sister. 'I'd spoken to director sahab yesterday and it seems there won't be a problem once we have the paperwork ready.'

'But what will the impact on the post-retirement pension be?' Mummy asked. 'There will be some impact on the pension, right?'

'I checked about that as well,' Bade Maama said. 'You will get Bhaisaab's pension even after you take the job. But since a government employee can avail only one dearness allowance, the pension's allowance will be cut.'

'So the pension will be halved, more or less,' Jagvir Chacha said.

'Yes.'

During the conversation and even after her uncles and aunties left, Gunjan felt pained by her ignorance. When were all these discussions happening? Why was she still someone who needed to be told these things by elders? They all said she needed to take care of her mother; but they had all gone about securing that *care* without involving her. Would it have been different if she were a son and not a daughter?

In the afternoon, after her bua had also left, Gunjan went up to Jagvir Chacha. 'So how do we start?'

'The death certificate,' he said. 'We will go to the municipal office tomorrow. You know where that is?'

'Yes.'

The municipal office compound consisted of a three-storey, red-painted building facing a ground that might once have been envisaged as a lush green lawn but had now turned into a parking lot of sorts. Gunjan remembered how she would take the road in front of the compound while going to and returning from the Holy Angels' Convent School, where she had studied all her school years. As a child, she had little idea what the building was for, or what work happened there. Once every year, she would see a big crowd of men congregate in the grounds, and at some point, she had learnt that all those men were seekers of rickshaw-pulling permits. She had found it strange that such a large office granted permits for something as simple as rickshaw-pulling.

Gunjan parked the Jetta in the grounds, between two diminutive Altos. She and her uncle entered the building corridors and asked for the office that issued death certificates. The men answering always stared at Gunjan, who was dressed in one of the two saris that her maami had left behind for her benefit. They were told that the office was at the rear of the building. There, the corridor branched off into a section that had three to four separate rooms along with a toilet that gave off a smell as bad as a morgue. Atop the door to the second room to their left, a board mentioned 'Birth/Death Registration'. Inside, they saw a single desk surrounded by four Muslim men (all had beards and caps). A road accident had killed five people of their family.

The stink from the toilet filled the room. Gunjan found it impossible to wait there and walked out into the corridor. Her uncle would manage the certificate, she thought. A bit farther ahead, the corridor opened to another small ground. There were some teenaged boys there, and a game of cricket was on. It was queer, Gunjan thought, that this was allowed during office hours; she drifted into watching the game. But the boys stopped at the sight of her. They looked curious, as if a novelty had entered their domain. Then, as if breaking from a still image that the entire group constituted, one of the boys came towards Gunjan, rubbed his crotch with his right hand and made an oohing sound. He then motioned as if he were holding a woman by the hips and taking her. Gunjan, repulsed, moved away. She heard the boys laugh behind her back. She retraced her steps and waited for Jagvir Chacha to come out with the damned certificate. The putrefying smell disturbed her; but she thought it would all end in a matter of minutes.

Jagvir Chacha came out pinching his nose. 'There is a small problem,' he said.

'What is it?' Gunjan asked.

'Here, see the doctor's note.'

She took the paper in her hand and looked at it. She had read it earlier; its contents included three punctuation-less sentences: *Mr Ranbir Singh 58 brought at 6 a.m. Unfortunately dead on arrival. Cause of death possible heart failure.* That morning, Gunjan's mother had found her father unresponsive and rushed to the neighbours for help. The neighbours, aware that he was dead already, had nevertheless taken her father's body to a heart specialist, who had handwritten this note on a letter. The same letter had to be produced at the municipal office to register the death and get the certificate.

'What's wrong with it?' she asked her uncle.

'Look at the date on top,' he said.

It was handwritten. 1 January 2014. It should have been 1 January 2015.

'Shit,' Gunjan said. 'Can't he just ignore it?'

'I asked him to. He says that his superiors weren't happy when he had made the same mistake last year. With the deaths of 1 January 2014.'

This meant that they would now have to go to the doctor and get a new note. It also meant that they would now get the certificate only tomorrow. All other processes could only start once the death certificate had been obtained.

The doctor's silly mistake, the rancid smell around the office, the fact that his uncle hadn't been able to understand the simple need for a bribe, the boy's offensive gesture – it all got to Gunjan. Something pent up bubbled over to the surface. On an impulse, she walked towards the place where the game of cricket was on. Her uncle followed her, confused.

Gunjan interrupted the game and walked towards the boy who had offended her. The boy just stood there dumbfounded. Gunjan grabbed his hair with her left hand and slapped him repeatedly with the right. Nobody moved till her uncle grabbed her and took her away. The boys were all stunned.

Gunjan was still shaking when they got into the car. 'What happened with those kids?' Chacha asked.

'That guy was making vulgar gestures at me.'

'You shouldn't get involved like this, beta.'

'I'm not a child anymore, Chachaji.'

Chacha didn't say anything to that. She reversed the car, took it outside the compound, and drove in the direction that would take them to the doctor's place. 'Sorry,' she said after a while.

At the doctor's, they were made to wait for almost an hour. When they eventually got to make the request, the doctor apologized for his mistake and wrote a new letter with the right date. He had a long face and kept a slim moustache and, with his expensive wrist watch and cuff-links, seemed somewhat too sophisticated for Muzaffarnagar. Gunjan had recognized him as the father of one of her best friends in Holy Angels' – Anjana. She had remembered the face from the parent–teacher meetings; only the hair had turned white. The connection felt too irrelevant to be brought up, and so she was pleasantly surprised when the doctor spoke: 'You are Gunjan, right?'

'Yes, Uncle. How do you know?'

'That episode? With the Muslim boy?'

Gunjan and Anjana had gone out on a secret double date once, a dangerous thing to do in Muzaffarnagar. The boys were from a different school, but they had been their classmates in Holy Angels' till Class X. The double-date consisted of nothing more than sharing a little snack at a joint in Mandi, but the consequences were terrible: Gunjan's date, a handsome guy named Daanish, was beaten up by some goons and was hospitalized. The goons had Gunjan and Anjana take a rickshaw and asked them to go to their homes. Looking back from that rickshaw was the last time she ever saw Daanish, and as she tried to remember his face now, she realized that she had forgotten him completely.

'You were with Anjana that day,' the doctor said.

Scared of being found out, she and Anjana had decided

never to talk about the day with anyone. So it took a moment for Gunjan to accept the doctor's assertion. 'I was with her, yes.'

'Your father and I had talked that time. Told each other to be more careful.'

It stunned Gunjan to know that her father had known of that disastrous adventure of her adolescent life and had never demanded an explanation from her. She now remembered that it had happened just before the board exams. Perhaps her father was saving her from the added stress.

'Thank you, Uncle,' she said, rising from her chair. Jagvir Chacha stood up too.

'I'm really sorry about your father, beta,' the doctor said.

As they were leaving his room, the doctor chipped in with a piece of advice: 'These days, the municipal office gives extra original death certificates for a fee. You should get many of those.'

'Yes, Uncle,' Gunjan said, hearing herself think that it was good advice.

In the car, Jagvir Chacha asked her about 'the episode with the Muslim boy' and she told him the facts. They drove homeward as the municipal office hours were over by then. It was only when they reached the farm that Gunjan realized that she hadn't asked Anjana's father about her friend's whereabouts.

After the evening tea, Gunjan's mother suggested that they look into her father's papers. She gave Jagvir Chacha the keys to the almirah where the papers were supposed to be, and withdrew to the kitchen, from where she shouted out to Gunjan after a few minutes.

In the kitchen, Gunjan's mother grabbed her arm and drew her closer. 'I want you to be present there,' she said in a voice of urgency. 'Next to the almirah. Be there and keep your eyes open. Your uncle will look into your father's papers. And your grandfather's papers. I trust him, but I can't understand a thing. You should. You should understand everything. Involve yourself, my child. Your father is gone now. There might be papers there related to your grandfather's properties. All that is still undivided. Unresolved. We took care of your grandfather till his death; not your uncles and their wives. You understand that? You understand what that means? You should know how much money the old man had. You should know how much money your father had. I haven't dealt with papers for thirty years now. But you've to understand what your rights are, what your inheritance is? Go, my child, stand by the almirah, look at all the papers. I have only you to trust.'

They found ten original death certificates for her grandfather, obtained by her father three days before his own death from the same municipal office that they had gone to. Her father had known that multiple original copies could be taken, Gunjan noted.

They found passbooks for seven bank accounts – two owned by her grandfather, four owned by her father, and one of them held jointly between her grandfather and father. 'This is the one into which the agricultural income comes,' Chacha said, leafing through the last passbook. Gunjan had never bothered to care if their family had any agricultural income, but it seemed logical since she knew that her grandfather owned some agricultural land. She could see that Jagvir Chacha was perturbed by the fact that her father jointly owned the account where that income accumulated. The fact that this account had the most money of all – nine lakhs – made the situation complicated. Should the money be divided equally among the families of all her grandfather's children? Or should 50 per cent of it come to her father's family, considering that her father held the account jointly? In none of her grandfather's accounts did the passbooks provide the names of any nominees, neither did her father's accounts mention an inheritor. 'This could be a problem,' Chacha said. Gunjan wondered why her grandfather's papers had not been looked into immediately after his death. Had her father prevented that? Or was it just that everyone expected they had more time?

They found two life insurance policy bonds belonging to her father along with annual premium payment receipts pinned neatly together to the last glossy page of the policies. The policies had been bought at the same time close to eight years ago. The last payments had been made in May of the previous year. 'Sum assured in either is three lakhs,' Chacha said. 'Here it says "payout is higher of sum assured or the fund value". So the minimum due is six lakhs.'

'Non-taxable,' he added after a minute. Tax was another thing to think of, Gunjan reminded herself.

They found a motor policy document for the scooter; the last premium had been paid a month ago.

They found a fat file that included all his salary slips, from up to three decades back. *Two hundred and fifty rupees*, Gunjan read in one of the oldest ones. In the same file, they found details of his provident fund, both the mandatory and voluntary ones. By his uncle's crude estimate, an amount between twenty to twenty-five lakhs had accumulated. That was Gunjan's father's life savings. That was how much he had managed. Had she been a conventional girl, a girl who sought an arranged marriage at the age of twenty-four, her father would have found it difficult to spend a lot on her marriage and have a comfortable retirement. By necessity, the marriage would have been a small affair: fifty people or so, little or no dowry, and a husband with pockmarks or a belly, or both.

*I am not rich*, Gunjan told herself loudly inside her head. *I have never been rich.*

They found brochures of some shares and mutual funds, not amounting to more than a lakh or so. Gunjan was the nominee in all of them.

They found two thousand-rupee notes in her father's wallet. Jagvir Chacha gave it to Gunjan. In her grandfather's wallet were four hundred-rupee notes. Jagvir Chacha gave the notes to Gunjan and kept the wallet separately. The rings worn by the men at the time of their death were also similarly managed – her father's ring given to Gunjan; her grandfather's ring kept separately, along with the wallet.

They found a little notebook in which was noted the money her father had lent to four of his friends in the city. It amounted to eighty thousand rupees.

They also found copies of the various applications her father had written to his office superiors. These were applications for availing privileged leave, applications to demand money for repairs to the many government residences granted to them over the years, applications to request withdrawals from his provident fund, applications for reimbursements for family medical expenses, and so on. The two applications for provident fund withdrawals named her as the reason – they corresponded to when she first went to Delhi for her bachelor's and when she got into a master's programme. Gunjan had never cared where her father got money from; and it had never occurred to her that it might have been better if she had paid it back. And, she remembered, she had asked her father for help with the advance when she had broken up with her first boyfriend and had to move to a flat of her own again. Her father had always paid, and she had never cared how.

'We should get the death certificates tomorrow, and start with all this,' Jagvir Chacha said, breaking her line of thought.

Around 10 p.m., lying alone in her room, Gunjan called Mahesh.

'Hey, how is it, love?' he asked.

'I'm alright,' she whispered. Mahesh knew that she had to speak like this.

'Hmm. What else?'

'I wanted to ask you one thing,' Gunjan said.

'Yes, what?'

'How much rent do the families pay? The other families who live in the building?'

'You mean in our building?' Mahesh asked.

'Yes, your building.'

'Umm ... Two point five lakhs per month. The ones on the ground floor pay a bit higher; I don't remember how much.'

'So if I were to pay for my stay with you, I would have to pay one point two five lakh?'

'Why would you pay to live with me?' said Mahesh, his voice strained.

'No, just saying.'

'Well, in that case, that's the calculation, yes.'

'You know my father's last salary was sixty thousand rupees. In hand.'

'Umm ... well, he was a government employee. The government doesn't pay much.'

'And my current salary,' Gunjan continued, 'it is sixty thousand too.'

'What's the point, baby? Why are you telling me this?'

'If I intended to pay rent to you, then that rent would be more than the total money coming into my family per month.'

'What happened, love? Why are you suddenly intent on feeling poor?'

'And you make more than twenty lakhs a month from rent alone? That's all my father's provident fund, right there.'

'What's the point, Gunjan?'

'Nothing, nothing really. I'm tired.'

'Take a deep sleep, baby. I will talk to you later.'

'Good night.'

The next morning, as Gunjan parked the car in the municipal office grounds, she saw two boys from the day before resting their cycles by the compound wall. They also saw her, and when she and Jagvir Chacha got out of the car, they ran away.

There was no game of cricket today, although the toilet next to the 'Birth/Death Registration' office still stank. Gunjan braved the smell and entered the room, followed by her uncle. There were two men sitting in front of the officer's desk, and they were having a conversation about state politics. Gunjan wondered how these men could indulge in idle talk in such hellish odour. She stood next to where the two men were seated and placed the letter from the doctor on the desk. The officer didn't notice it, but then Gunjan placed a thousand-rupee note above the letter. 'I want ten death certificates for my father,' she said. The officer looked up at her. 'It's best if you can manage this in the next ten-fifteen minutes.' The officer nodded towards the other men and they vacated their chairs for Gunjan and Jagvir Chacha. 'Thank you, but we will stand outside,' Gunjan said, swatting the air around her nose.

'Okay, madam,' the officer said.

Standing outside, Gunjan's mind rested a brief moment on the irony of the fact that the thousand-rupee note she had used was from her father's wallet. Jagvir Chacha stood silently next to her, shifting his weight between his legs. In the grounds next to their standing space, there was still no game of cricket.

After ten minutes, the officer came out of the room with the required papers. As he handed them over, he said, 'Cancer in the summer, and heart attacks in the winters. So many deaths, madam. Are you the daughter?'

Gunjan took the certificates and ignored the question.

'Yes, she is the daughter,' Jagvir Chacha answered the officer. 'And I'm the brother.'

'Your bhaisaab was so blessed,' the officer responded to Chacha, 'to have such a beautiful daughter.'

'Let's go to the bank,' Gunjan said to Chacha.

As they walked towards to the car, they saw a group of boys near the compound gate, racing away on their cycles. When they reached the spot where the car was parked, they saw that the car had been vandalized. Someone had scrawled something on the hood, with a metal key or some other pointed instrument. It took only a moment's concentration to read what was written: रंडी. *Whore.*

'I told you not to get involved,' Jagvir Chacha said.

Gunjan didn't say anything and got into the car.

'Whose car is it?' Chacha asked once inside the car.

'My friend's.'

'You'll now have to spend money on it.'

Gunjan switched on the ignition. 'This town is shit.' she said. 'Shit. Shit. Shit. Shit. Shit.'

---

At the first branch they visited, they were told that Gunjan's father's account there had no nominees specified. This meant that the money could not be transferred to Gunjan or her mother directly. The branch manager that Gunjan and her uncle met – a bald man with Gandhi specs and a turtleneck sweater beneath his blazer – seemed to find pleasure in conveying the technical complications. He invited them to his cabin and asked an attendant to bring in three cups of tea. He was in no hurry.

'Earlier, it was not necessary to mention nominees while opening a bank account,' the branch manager said. 'There wasn't much awareness, you could say. But things have changed completely in the last ten years or so. Lately, we have reached out to all our account holders regarding this. Through SMS. Specifying nominees is mandatory now. And it saves a lot of problems if an account holder dies. But your father must have been busy, or maybe our messages didn't reach him. Earlier, people didn't have mobile phone numbers registered with their bank accounts, too, so we might not have had his number with us. I presume he didn't use Internet banking.'

'So what's the procedure now?' Gunjan asked the manager.

'To receive the account holder's money, the heirs need to get a certificate,' the manager said. 'It's issued by the district administration.'

'I don't understand,' Gunjan said.

'It's simple. The fact that you and your mother are the only heirs needs to be stamped by the district administration. For that, they will need affidavits from three people.'

'What should these affidavits say?' Jagvir Chacha asked.

'That Madam and Mataji are indeed the heirs of Mr Ranbir Singh.'

'Okay,' Gunjan said. 'So we just give a copy of that certificate to you, then?'

'There is more,' the manager said.

'What?'

'Each bank that Mr. Ranbir Singh has an account in will need to know to whom his money needs to be transferred. Now, our bank would not want to be involved in a future dispute between the heirs. What I'm saying is simple: since there are two heirs in this case, one of you will have to provide an affidavit saying that you are fine with the other person receiving the full sum. Unless there is a conflict that you are aware of. In which case things get more complicated.'

'There is no conflict,' Jagvir Chacha said. 'Her mother should get the money.'

'If that is the case, Madam will have to sign an affidavit conveying the same,' the manager said, pointing towards Gunjan. He took off his specs and wiped the lens with his handkerchief. Everything about him seemed rehearsed and, for that reason, Gunjan didn't like him. 'There has to be a different affidavit for each bank,' he added, 'and each affidavit needs to have the exact details of the concerned accounts.'

'Understood, *Sir*,' Gunjan said.

Over the day, as they went to the branches of other banks, one after the other, they realized that the situation with each account was the same, including her grandfather's accounts and the joint account between her father and her grandfather.

There were no nominees specified, and this meant that affidavits and certificates would be required for each. Gunjan and Jagvir Chacha agreed that it was prudent to focus on her father's accounts first. The effort required to get the heir certificates for her grandfather's accounts was a problem that seemed beyond their capacity at this time.

That evening, there was nothing to do. From the verandah, Gunjan noticed a dense fog engulfing the house. Her mother was in her bedroom, knitting something for Chhoti Maami's younger son, who was four years old. Jagvir Chacha was in the living room, watching the news with the volume really low, so that the neighbours wouldn't know that the TV was on. The murmur of the TV somehow added to the silence, and the house sounded like a place that had been abandoned.

Mahesh called, but Gunjan didn't pick up. She did not want to talk to him right now. In front of her eyes, in the backyard, the white fog settled slowly like a viscous thing. Owing to the silence in the house, Gunjan sometimes felt that the fog was making a sound. She felt a gnawing emptiness otherwise. She could not, however, attribute this mood of hers to the fact of her father's death. It wasn't that simple. Perhaps it was something that was adrift in her own self that was forming these thoughts. But how could she know whether these perceptions were shared by the others as well? Yes, she strongly sensed the desolation of the house, but there was no objective way to communicate it to, or discuss its possible causes with, her mother or her uncle.

She opened the gate to her left and went into the backyard and inhaled the fog. Then she sat on her bicycle and pedalled forward. She made a tiny circle, and then another. She kept circling, enjoying the silly idea that her movement was cleaving the fog.

The morning of the next day, 7 January, Gunjan and Jagvir Chacha went to the branch of a private life insurance company. Gunjan's mother, a nominee in one of the policies, was with them. Gunjan made her take the rear seat so that she couldn't see the word scrawled on the front.

The operations person at the branch asked them for the doctor's note along with the death certificate.

'But that note was taken by the municipal office,' Jagvir Chacha said.

'It is normally needed to show that the death was natural,' the man said.

'We can get a new note from the doctor,' said Gunjan. She smiled briefly at the man, who seemed her age. 'But it would be great if you can spare us the trouble.'

'I'll file the claim,' the man said, smiling back. 'Sometimes, the head-office people decide to do an investigation. These policies are of a small amount; so they likely won't care. But it's also true that there have been a lot of frauds in Muzaffarnagar. So the company is cautious.'

'That's why we are giving two *original* death certificates,' Gunjan said. 'They will be convinced there is no fraud.' Gunjan had realized the importance of those documents just before saying that.

The man then collected the identification documents, along with the bank account information, from them. He filed the claims in the system. Gunjan's mind was stuck on how easily this man had called the policies 'of a small amount'. It occurred to her that she did not have life insurance. Then she wondered how big Mahesh's insurance policy must be.

'How long will it take to get the money?' Gunjan's mother asked the man.

'If there is smooth processing, Auntyji, the money should be in your bank account in seven working days.'

After the claim-filing, they went to drop Jagvir Chacha to the railway station. He was to catch a train to Ambala, where he lived with his wife (both his children were in college). At the platform, he took Gunjan's mother's hands in his, touched them with his forehead, and sobbed a couple of times. His train was late, but he insisted that Gunjan and her mother not wait with him. 'Go to the tehsil office,' he said to Gunjan just before they left.

Gunjan dropped her mother home and then drove to the tehsil office. There was a main building in the centre of the compound, and all around in the open ground surrounding it, countless shops and shacks and desks had been set up. The din of the numerous typewriters at work was adding a busy music to the air. Apart from the odd woman trailing behind her husband, the place was full of men. The small and big establishments belonged to lawyers, stamp sellers, notary officers, and hangers-on – all of them making a living out of giving this or that service to people caught in administrative tangles, the kind Gunjan and her mother had found themselves in with respect to the bank accounts. Half of the shops were operated by Muslims, the others by Hindus, and the crowd distributed itself accordingly. As Gunjan stood at a spot, stunned by the hustle-bustle around her, she wished she could avoid this bureaucratic excess.

At random, she picked a tiny shop, a Muslim lawyer's place, and stood at the entrance. Inside, four men sat on a single bench, facing a desk, behind which the lawyer sat working on a computer.

'Hi, Mr Syed,' she said in English. She had read the name on the board above the entrance.

The lawyer looked up from his keyboard, crinkled his eyebrows, and went back to his typing for a second. Then he looked up again and said, 'Please, Madam, come inside.'

Gunjan entered the place, which was not more than sixty–seventy square feet of space. She stood next to the bench and inside half a minute the four men vacated it and stood outside the shop.

'What I can do for you, please?' the lawyer asked.

Gunjan switched to Hindi and explained the bank account situation to the lawyer. The four men standing outside were joined by a few more.

Having understood the situation, the lawyer said, 'Heir certificates are granted by the magistrate. It can take up to six months.'

'Six months!' said Gunjan.

'Yes. If you go by the normal route,' the lawyer said. He then looked to the small crowd that had assembled outside his shop. The men began to shift away. After the last curious person had left, he said, 'The file goes through four levels. And there are rates decided at each level. It can happen in a month; but it would cost thirty thousand rupees.'

Gunjan nodded. After a second, she said, 'I will discuss with my mother. There are also other affidavits. For other things. Like my mother's application for a job in my father's department. On compassionate grounds.'

'Yes,' the lawyer said. 'You will need to sign an affidavit saying that you don't want that job.'

'How long does that take?' Gunjan said.

The lawyer laughed. 'You have no experience of these things,' he said.

'My father can only die once,' Gunjan replied curtly.

'No, no, please don't take it badly. I mean you don't have any experience of signing affidavits, etc. I will arrange the stamp papers and get the language ready for you. If you can give me all details right now, it will be done by four in the afternoon.'

Gunjan gave him a paper with the details of all tasks that required affidavits. 'Still, how much does it take?' she asked.

'Fifty rupees per affidavit,' the lawyer answered. 'I will also need passport-sized photographs – yours and your mother's.'

'Here,' Gunjan passed on the photos. 'Thank you,' she said, and stood up from the bench. 'I will be back at four.'

'Okay, Madam,' said the lawyer.

As she was moving further from the shop and into the general pandemonium, a man of about forty years, dressed in a white kurta–pyjama, approached her. 'Madam,' he said.

'Yes?'

'I heard that you've some trouble with your father's money,' he said.

'Yes, apparently there are bribes needed,' Gunjan said.

'Yes, thirty thousand is the going rate here for all such requests,' the man said.

'Can you help?' Gunjan asked.

'You don't know this, Madam, but branch managers have a monetary limit up to which they can accept such transfers without seeking the heir certificate,' the man said. 'Your money can come to you inside a day.'

'I talked to four branch managers today. Not one told me of any such limit,' said Gunjan.

'They won't because they want money,' the man said.

'But if they want money, they've to at least suggest that such a way exists,' Gunjan said. Then, after a moment, 'Why are you helping me?'

'Madam, this is the thing I do,' the man said. 'For five thousand rupees per account, I will talk to all your branch managers and they will transfer the money without any problem. Just that the money in each account should be less than five lakhs.'

The money in each of his father's accounts was less than five lakhs. Gunjan was impressed with such entrepreneurship. This man was offering her a deal better than the thirty thousand that Mr Syed had offered. And it would be faster. 'I can't pay before I get the money,' Gunjan said.

'Okay, no problem,' the man said.

'I will come back around four,' she said. 'Can I tell you then?'

'Okay, okay, you will meet me around this area only,' the man said.

'Yes. Thank you for the offer. What's your name?'

'Madam, Mr Syed anyway won't give you the best advice,' the man said. 'My name is Jairam; it's my duty to help women like you.'

'Women like me?'

'You came in a big car, Madam. Jetta. Surely you can't be bothered with five–six lakh rupees for too long. And why should you go to a Muslim lawyer?'

A heat rose from her throat and suffused her whole face. She looked away from the man and moved away from the conversation. He had been following her right from the parking lot, she realized.

'See you at four, Madam,' the man said behind her back.

Walking towards the parking lot, Gunjan felt a clenching of her jaws. The car didn't fit with what this town was. It gave people wrong ideas about her, about who she was and what she could afford. And it vexed her further that the Hindu–Muslim card should be pulled on her.

---

At home, Gunjan explained the situation to her mother.

'We should give the money to this Jairam fellow and get everything sorted quickly,' her mother said. 'The insurance money will come soon, right?'

'Mummy, I have the amount we need for Jairam,' Gunjan said.

'I can pay you back from the insurance money, then.'

'You don't worry about it, Mummy,' Gunjan said. 'Don't.'

Her mother smiled, and then proceeded towards the kitchen to prepare lunch. Gunjan noticed how her hair was unkempt, dishevelled. Her mother had aged inside a week. She'd been a beautiful woman, and still was, but it was as if she had committed herself to the image of the widow. For a moment, Gunjan wondered if her parents had had a sex life. And if they did, what all of this meant for her mother. In India, and more so in Muzaffarnagar, it was not possible for her to seek a male companion at her age.

With her daughter working in Delhi, visiting her frequently at first and less and less over time, would this woman be condemned to a loneliness extending right till her death?

Now, sitting alone in the living room, Gunjan speculated about the future. Her mother would be asked to vacate the bungalow in another three months. But the mess with the documents and the money would clear much before that. So her mother would get a clerical job on compassionate grounds and would move to a small flat in the farm residential colony. Another year or more down the line, she would leave Mahesh and start living by herself. None of these outcomes seemed desirable to her: her mother becoming a working woman after thirty years of homemaking; her mother moving to a much smaller place; and she herself, thirty years old, tired of men, dealing with a hostile Delhi alone – a Bridget Jones in a rapacious city.

She thought of all the harassment she had faced in Delhi as a woman. With her first boyfriend, getting groped on a DTC bus in his presence left them both feeling helpless, and that was part of the reason why they separated. She learnt driving from her second boyfriend, who owned an old Maruti Alto. But her weekday commute was still something she had to manage on public transport. Then came Mahesh.

She sometimes wondered if she had accepted Mahesh's affections because of the safety implicit in his company, whereby she seldom had to take public transport and even otherwise stood behind an invisible wall of class, with the lecherous side of Delhi denied access to her. There were, however, notable reminders even on the right side of the wall. A couple of Mahesh's friends had slapped her behind in parties, in a manner so nonchalant that she had wondered if this was a casual way of acknowledging someone among the rich and had not, therefore, told Mahesh anything. Once, at a reception party they had attended, the drunk groom had danced so suggestively with her that the bride had had to intervene. It had been particularly embarrassing for Gunjan, for the bride's accusing eyes had blamed her for not abstaining from the dance.

Gunjan went to the kitchen and hugged her mother from behind. 'How will you manage everything, Mummy?' she asked.

'Things will work out,' her mother said, and turned to face her.

'I wanted to ask you how ... how do you feel about working?'

'I don't know what it'll be like,' her mother said. 'I've only read *Grihshobha* and *Kadambini* after my B.A. Not even the newspapers. The last time I dealt seriously with books was when I could still help you with homework.'

'Does it scare you?' Gunjan asked.

'A bit. But I'm more scared about you.'

'About me?'

'Yes,' Mother said walking towards the sink to wash some carrots. 'Whose car is it?'

'I told you,' said Gunjan. 'My friend's.'

'Such a big car. And he's given it to you for so many days. Must be a special friend.'

Gunjan shrugged.

'Someone scratched something on it?'

'Yes, some loafers at the municipal office. Chachaji was there.'

'Aren't you going to have to pay for this?'

'I'll manage, Mummy,' Gunjan said. 'It's something I can manage.'

The pressure cooker gave a whistle. Gunjan could sense her mother's discomfort with the car, and she herself had seen how it created problems. 'I'll stop taking out the car from now on,' she said.

'What sort of life do you have, child?' her mother asked, as if the question flowed naturally from the context of their conversation. 'Do you realize,' she added, 'that I don't even know where you live in Delhi? Your father never knew that either, and it used to make him anxious.'

'I live in Vasant Vihar,' Gunjan said. 'With a roommate.'

Her mother just kept looking at her.

'And I have a good life,' said Gunjan, evading her mother's eyes.

Her mother nodded, sighed. Then she said, 'Good that you won't take the car. But what will you do? The scooter doesn't start easily. You'll have to hail rickshaws each time.'

Gunjan took a moment, then said, 'I'll take the cycle.'

Her mother laughed. 'Like your school days?'

Gunjan laughed too. 'Why don't you go watch a serial?' she said then. 'I will make the chapattis.'

'You know how to make chapattis?' her mother asked, feigning a wide-eyed look of surprise.

'Of course I do, Madam. My mummy taught me.'

---

Around 3 p.m., Gunjan took off her salwar and slipped on her black slacks. She then wiped the cycle clean with an old rag: with the nightly dew, stipples of dust had gathered over its entire frame. It was in perfect shape otherwise. She sat on it and pedalled away.

In fifteen minutes, she was near the tehsil office. The sun

had shone brightly that day and there was still some warmth in the air. She felt refreshed with the exercise and left the cycle some distance away from the main gate.

Inside the compound, Mr Syed was ready with the affidavits. They had been notarized even before being signed by Gunjan or her mother, which, Gunjan noted, wasn't exactly the right practice. She paid him the money and walked away from the shop.

A few paces ahead, she saw Jairam. He waved to her.

'We will do it tomorrow?' she said.

'Okay, Madam,' he said.

Gunjan nodded and made to walk past him. Just then, Jairam said, 'Madam, where do you live? Outside India somewhere? America?'

'Jairamji,' Gunjan paused, 'I'll use your help to get my father's money and I'll pay you for that. And that's it. We don't have to talk about anything else.'

'Okay, Madam, okay.' He smiled sheepishly.

Gunjan walked away, found her cycle, and pedalled homewards. She did not want to deal with this man and she did not want to pay him any money. There had to be a way to get around him.

In the evening, she called Mahesh and told him about the damage to his car. She did not tell him the exact word the rascals at the municipal office had scrawled on the bonnet, though.

'Don't worry, baby,' Mahesh said. 'It's nothing. I'll take care of the car. Just ... let me know if you have any idea when things might be under control in Muzaffarnagar.'

'There is still a lot of work here,' she said.

'I know, I know. It's just that I'm missing you.'

'How are you passing your evenings?'

'Nothing much. By the way, I had someone reach out to your boss and tell him that he shouldn't expect you for at least another week.'

'That's right,' Gunjan said. 'Thanks.'

'It's alright, love. I love you.'

'You are so nice to me,' Gunjan said.

'Do you love me, baby? You've not forgotten about me, have you?'

'I have not,' Gunjan said. 'But there is a lot going on here.'

'You can say the three words at least,' Mahesh said.

'Alright. I love you,' she said, and heard Mahesh sigh at the other end.

'I'm worried about my mother,' she said. 'She is going to be alone.'

'We will discuss things when you get here. We will discuss the future.'

'Hmm ... alright. Sorry about the car again, Mahesh.'

'Not an issue, Gunjan, not an issue.'

After she cut the call, she thought of the future Mahesh was referring to. Would he propose to her? Would she be able to say yes? Or no? She'd never thought of herself as the sort of woman who would marry for anything other than love. And what she had for Mahesh was not much more than affection. She'd loved her first boyfriend and it had been painful separating from him. But it had seemed necessary at the point. Perhaps she should have stuck with him; married him, even.

Gunjan had seen her father's dead body in the toilet-cum-bathroom that had been modified for her grandfather's use. Since then, she had taken to using the other toilet, the Indian-style one just outside her room. But, accustomed to the Western-style toilets that she used in Delhi, she had some trouble adjusting to the squatting routine for the first couple of days. It was a peculiar, private adjustment, for it was also true that for the first seventeen years of her life, when she was growing up with her parents, she had only ever used Indian-style toilets. In fact, this bungalow, with its two toilets, one of which had been modified to house a Western-style pot, had been allotted to her father only after his last promotion three years ago. Before this, their family had lived in three different apartments in the colony, progressing from two-room to three-room to four-room housing as her father got promoted every five to six years. None of those apartments had more than one Indian-style toilet. Gunjan had lived all her schoolgoing years in those three places, and her morning routine in the later years usually included attempts at being the first one to use the toilet; for somehow, either due to the commodes' shape or due to the ineffectiveness of the exhaust fan, the shit smell lingered. However, she could not act on her preference much, for her father always woke up first; and so it happened rather often that Gunjan got to use the toilet after him. On such days, she would pinch her nose before entering the toilet and, creating a look of disgust on her face, say something like 'such great digestion!' or 'smells like the end of the world'. These enactments, never serious, would be meant for her mother only, who always laughed loudly and tried to hush Gunjan at the same time. Her father would ignore this mother–daughter silliness.

Over the first two or three days after her father's death,

Gunjan's re-initiation to Indian-style toilets had brought to her mind a particular comparison. At Mahesh's house, the two toilets needed the word *exquisite* to describe them. Even the flush made a pleasing, self-effacing sort of sound. There, you could be drunk, half-asleep or immersed in your phone: the downstairs business more or less took care of itself. Here, in Muzaffarnagar, the toilet was basic, even brutal. The up-close view of your excreta, the unavoidable smell, and the strenuous squatting posture – all ensured that you didn't linger in the place. The flushing normally failed, such that an extra bucket of water often needed to be used.

Slowly, though, as the days had passed, Gunjan had adapted. Going to the toilet wasn't a bothersome idea anymore. She did not have to place her palm on the wall to find her balance as she squatted; her knees did not make an awful, clicking sound when she stood up after finishing her business; her feet did not go numb after the whole experience. Although she could not take her phone inside (for fear of dropping it), her mind had begun to use the private space to think of a thing or two.

On the morning of 8 January, seven days after her father's death, Gunjan found herself thinking of her lack of grief while squatting in the toilet. She had already shat; she was lingering. It was then that it hit her – the smell. The smell of her own shit.

She filled water in the toilet mug to wash herself and saw it shake in her hands. After she was done, she got out of the toilet and, while in front of the washbasin in the verandah, absent-mindedly dabbed the liquid soap bottle much more than needed. The excessive lather drew her attention. She saw a flash of her father shaving right at the spot where she was standing. She looked up at the mirror above the washbasin, and for a minute tried to match her father's facial features with her own. She then went to the bathroom and lifted a bucket of water, using it to flush the toilet. Again she smelled her shit. The man had died and she was alive and here it was, the connection. After only three days of eating food cooked by her mother. Her insides, her intestines, her body – all a testament. She collapsed on the floor just outside the toilet and let out a shriek, which brought her mother rushing to her. 'What happened?' Gunjan was asked.

But she was choked with emotion and could not speak. Her mother tried to lift her but, as soon as she stood up, she crumbled again, as if paralyzed. 'What is wrong, my child?' her mother asked with a strain in her voice. Gunjan coughed, grunted, mumbled. Her face was smeared with tears. 'You thinking of Papa?' Gunjan raised her eyes to meet her mother's. Then she cried again. A cascade. Her mother raised her face to her chest.

They stayed in that position right outside the toilet for a few minutes. Then they moved to the bedroom, where Gunjan lay down on the bed. Her mother sat next to her.

'Don't cry like this, my child,' Mummy said. 'Your father, he's up there somewhere. Imagine how sad it will make him to see you like this.'

Gunjan noticed that her mother's tone was different, as if she were talking to a child. 'It's because I'd not cried till now,' she said, still hiccupping from the exertion. She wiped her face with her hands. 'I'm going to get everything sorted, Mummy,' she said then. 'We will get the money, you'll get the job, and you'll get a good apartment to shift to.'

They were silent after that. Fifteen minutes or so later, Mummy went to the kitchen to toast bread for breakfast. Gunjan had a twitchy nap on the bed, a nap that allowed for thoughts. Her father had died and there was bureaucracy and she was running through the motions. She had to stop going through the motions and beat the bureaucracy and ensure that her father's death didn't become the ruin of them.

Mother and daughter had breakfast in the living room. After that, Gunjan put some papers in a polythene bag, knotted the bag around the cycle's handle, and left the house.

She went straight to the bank branch where the manager, wearing the same turtleneck sweater he had been wearing three days ago, greeted her into his cabin.

'I met a man at the tehsil office,' Gunjan said, coming straight to the point. 'His name was Jairam. Do you know him?'

'I don't know any Jairam, Ma'am,' the manager said, shifting a coaster on his side of the table between them. 'Why?' he asked.

'I got to know that you have the power to release the money in my father's account without insisting on a certificate,' Gunjan said.

'Who told you that?' the manager said.

'This Jairam did.'

'Well, Ma'am, anyone on the street can tell you anything. What I told you last time was procedure. I can't release the money without following procedure. No bank can. You can talk to other branch managers if you want.'

'That's strange,' Gunjan said. 'Because this Jairam offered to talk to you on my behalf and have the money released.'

'Nonsense,' the manager said.

'He wanted a fee, of course,' Gunjan said. 'He said that he would talk to all the different banks for me.'

'I don't know any Jairam–Phairam,' the manager said, his eyes searching outside the glass panel in his cabin, as if seeking help.

'Look here, bhaisaab,' Gunjan said, shocking the man into a wide-eyed stare. 'You and your fellow branch managers are running a racket. It works fine as long as it's some villager who leaves his sons clueless about the money in the farming account. You take a bribe from one of the sons and use your … your discretionary powers to transfer the money to him. Works just fine. The rest are so poor and clueless, they don't know what hit them.'

'How can you refer to me like that?' the manager growled. He actually used the English word 'refer'.

'My only thing, bhaisaab,' Gunjan went on, 'don't do it with me. You probably thought it's just two women – mother and daughter – and they will not know what to do. No, I'm going to post this whole story on Facebook. *And* I'm going to call your bank's head office in Mumbai and report this. *And* I'm going to go to the police. *And* report this to whatever news channel I can find. *And*, because it's two helpless women against a corrupt banking system, fighting for a government employee's hard-earned money, *everyone* will listen.'

'You're trying to scare me?' the manager said, a mixture of anger and fear in his voice. 'I told you procedure and you're trying to scare me?'

'You don't need to be scared,' Gunjan replied. 'You just need to do something that is within your powers. Can I, please, have the money transferred by tomorrow?'

The manager moved a palm over his bald pate. 'Your threats …' he said, then used the pause to look sideways, 'how can I be sure?'

'Here's the filled form,' Gunjan said, pushing a paper

towards him. 'My mother's account details are on it. I've also put my affidavit under it. This is all the paperwork you need. You don't need that stupid heir certificate from the magistrate's office.'

'But how can I be sure, Ma'am,' the manager took the documents and examined them, 'that you won't do those things you mentioned?'

'Have the money transferred by tomorrow,' Gunjan said. 'Also, talk to the other branch managers and tell them to do the same. I'll go to them right after this and give them the papers one by one.'

'The other managers won't listen to me,' the manager said.

'You've to convince them,' Gunjan said with finality and rose from the seat. 'Call them after I leave. They should know the situation before I meet them.'

---

Gunjan didn't need to intimidate the other branch managers. They all accepted her papers and grunted 'yes' when asked about managing the money transfers. In between, while she was cycling from bank to bank, Gunjan was scared of what these men could do in retaliation. At one point, she stopped her cycle and called Mahesh, telling him all about the conversation with the bald branch manager. It was an act of creating witness. Mahesh laughed. He also advised her to tell her mother, which Gunjan knew was a bad idea and thus rejected.

The strategy with the bald branch manager had come to her in the morning, while she was slowing her cycle outside the tehsil office. She had realized that she didn't want to deal with Jairam and, in the spirit of cutting the middleman, she assessed whether she already had enough information to enforce the outcome that she wanted.

Her resolve outside the tehsil office and the toilet episode in the morning – they were somehow related. Something latent in her had been released this morning, due to the knowledge that her connection with her father was immitigable – that even if her mind let go of him, her body could never do so. An intensity had been added to the part of her character that was responding to the situations that had arisen after her father's death. He himself had always been a gentle man, unable to intimidate anyone. Gunjan had, on the other hand, bared the ferocity that her own life had taught her.

As she cycled homeward, she thought of how her going away from Muzaffarnagar to Delhi had primarily been a movement away from a small town to a bigger one, the kind of movement that everyone from her generation (and education) in Muzaffarnagar had to undertake. But over the years, her settling into a life in Delhi had taken her away from the otherwise important people in her life, the ones who had continued to live in Muzaffarnagar – her parents. She remembered how in the first couple of years she would visit them every weekend. That frequency had decreased gradually, and at the time of her grandfather's and father's death, she was in the habit of visiting home for no more than the annual holidays of Holi and Diwali. Her aspirations had been all about improving what she had come to see as her lifestyle. There was no element of giving anything back to her parents, for that would have meant a return to Muzaffarnagar – a mental return, if not a physical one. She would have had to think of her parents, and thinking of her parents would have meant thinking of the kind of life they had in Muzaffarnagar. And Muzaffarnagar was a town that she had conditioned herself to think of as an incidental occurrence, not a permanence of her life.

But wasn't Muzaffarnagar a permanent part of her life's story? She thought of this question as she pedalled past the railway station on her left. The winter sun was strong and clear. When she took the less busy Circular Road, she saw how the slow movements of the town could be mistaken for beauty. Didn't she already think of Delhi's hustle-bustle as a sort of ugliness? Mahesh's money had insulated her from that ugliness, but wasn't that money the most impermanent part of her life?

For her, her grandfather's death had been a tiny vacation from work. Everyone in her family had expected it, and she had assumed that everyone was partly relieved. But her father was sad. He was the only son willing to take care of the old man, although it had never been clear if his dedication was a product of love. Could it be that love and filial duty were enmeshed for her father, that he didn't know where one ended and the other began? And was the converse true for her – that because she had never felt, or been made to feel, the pull of duty, she had also forgotten about love?

As she neared home, these questions receded to the background and the concerns of the here and now rose up again. She measured how much work she had completed. The insurance money could come any day now, and the bank money, she hoped, would get sorted soon. The provident fund money and the insurance money from the department her father worked for required no active intervention. The only thing left was filing the application for her mother's job. She had already prepared the affidavits required for the same.

As she was crossing the director's bungalow, it occurred to her that it was lunch time and that her father's erstwhile boss might be inside his house. She left her cycle by the curated bushes outside the bungalow and walked inside.

The door was opened by the director's wife. 'Namaste, Aunty,' Gunjan said, 'is Uncle home?'

'Yes, yes,' the woman said, 'please come inside. Have you had lunch?'

'Oh, yes, Aunty,' Gunjan said. 'I just wanted to talk to Uncle about my mother's job.'

There was a courtyard inside, girt by an L-shaped verandah on two sides. The director was having his lunch seated in the courtyard, taking in the sun. He smiled looking at Gunjan, pointed towards the couple of plastic chairs scattered around him. Gunjan pulled one of them and sat opposite him.

'I'm sorry to bother you at lunch, Uncle,' Gunjan said.

'No worries, beta. Please have lunch with me.'

'No, thanks, Uncle. I just came to ask a few questions.'

'Yes, tell me.'

'So … this is about my mother's possible appointment … on compassionate grounds. My uncle had a chat with you about this earlier.'

'Yes, he did. I'd explained the procedure to him.'

'Yes,' Gunjan said. 'I just wanted to know … how will things pan out? When will she get the job? What will she get? What sort of housing?'

The director nodded, then washed his fingers over his steel plate. It was a practice Gunjan detested. Looking at the yellow–red water collect itself in the utensils, she suddenly remembered how she had made her father give up this habit when she was in sixth or seventh grade. This speck of memory surprised her, pleasantly.

'Right,' the director said. 'Your chacha told me that bhabhiji is a graduate. In Hindi.'

'Yes, Uncle, that's right.'

'See, this practice,' he took a moment to wipe his fingers on a hand towel kept on his plastic chair, 'this practice of giving jobs on compassionate grounds is an old one, and isn't appreciated much today.'

'Why is that?'

'It upsets those who are already in the department. It's natural for them to think that women who get such jobs don't deserve them.'

'So ... but it's a rule, right?' Gunjan asked.

'Not really,' the director said. 'It's discretionary and dependent on availability, though I have seldom seen such requests denied by the headquarters. It takes about three months, which should work fine in your case. I'm letting bhabhiji keep the house at least till June.'

'Oh, thank you, Uncle,' Gunjan said, an immediate concern of hers erased.

'But what we can offer,' the director said, 'considering that she's a graduate from an unrelated subject, is a low-level clerical position. Support staff, basically.'

'What would this mean?' Gunjan asked.

'Making photocopies, making sure the tea bills are signed and paid off, passing files,' he said.

Gunjan absorbed this, imagining her mother doing all this in her fifties. Her father's peon, Sukhiram, did all this for him. He also ran errands for her father, even helping him sell his produce from the kitchen garden at times. 'A peon?' she asked, looking down to the floor.

'She's an ex-officer's wife,' the director said. 'I'm sure her colleagues will keep that in mind. She won't be overworked.'

Gunjan nodded.

'I know how this can feel awkward,' the director said. 'But

there is going to be a pay commission revision. The salary will be attractive at this level too. And Ranbirji's pension will also increase.'

There was something else on Gunjan's mind now. She knew that peons in the department usually got one-room housing. She couldn't imagine her mother living there, as a neighbour to Sukhiram. Their relatives' shame alone would make that option not viable. So her mother would need to take a place on rent in the town. But then she would have to commute in a rickshaw every day. It would be a hassle. 'Isn't there a way that the housing granted can be of a higher grade?' Gunjan asked the director, already sensing how silly her query sounded.

'No,' the director said. 'Even if I granted it, some or the other employee will complain.'

'Okay,' Gunjan said. She had to tell all this to her mother. She now worried that her mother would accept this life so that her daughter could remain free in Delhi. Thinking of this made her throat tighten. She stood up from the chair and mumbled a 'thank you' to the director.

She had just turned towards the verandah when the director said, 'Why don't you take the job, Gunjan?'

'What do you mean, Uncle?' Gunjan asked.

'I'd told your uncle about it,' the director said. 'He told me that you wouldn't want the job.'

'If it's being a peon ...' Gunjan shrugged.

'Sit down,' the director said, pointing towards the chair Gunjan had just vacated. 'You've a masters' degree, right?'

'Yes, I do,' Gunjan said, sitting down.

'Then, by very precedent, you can't be a peon,' he said. 'You'll start a grade higher. And your degree is in marketing, right?'

'Umm ... mass communications.' Gunjan said.

'And years of experience?'

'Almost six.'

The director took a deep breath and leaned back on his chair. 'I could make a case for your inclusion in a high grade. No marketing talent wants to work in government jobs. But we too have our events, our outreach campaigns with farmers in the community.'

'What would it mean? Salary? Housing?' Gunjan asked.

'You'll have to leave the bungalow. But you can retain a two-bedroom flat here. I can push for that. A promotion would take a long time, though.'

'Salary?'

'Umm ...' he went into thought. 'I think all combined it'll be around forty thousand in your hand. But, as I said, there's a pay commission due.'

Sixty thousand in Delhi versus forty thousand in Muzaffarnagar – this was Gunjan's first thought. She didn't want to say yes or no right now. 'I'll ... I'll tell you whatever we decide, Uncle. I'll talk to my mother.'

'And, yes, half of your father's pension will reach you each month.'

Adding the pension, their total income would be close to sixty thousand. Gunjan got up from the seat and, after a few moments in which her mind considered that option and what it could mean, found herself outside the director's bungalow. It took her a whole minute to find her cycle. As she took it out of the bush, the lawns where her father's and grandfather's terahvi had taken place appeared before her eyes. And then, on the road between her and the lawns, she saw the stooped figure of her grandfather. He was on a slow walk, the kind he would take even two winters back.

She remembered how her mother had told her that till the time the old man walked, death couldn't touch him. Slowly, her grandfather passed her by, without looking at her. Behind him, turning from the perpendicular road that led to their bungalow, came her father, sitting atop the same cycle whose handle she was holding in her hands. He was in his trademark attire – a chequered shirt with its sleeves folded, untucked above black trousers. He pedalled slowly, as if he had something on his mind. Just when he was crossing her, he looked in her direction and smiled.

It was as if he approved of the idea.

Gunjan started walking homeward, pulling the cycle beside her. As she turned towards the bungalow, the parked Jetta came into sight. She came close to it and saw the obscenity scrawled on its bonnet. This town is shit, she thought, and smiled.

# *Acknowledgements*

I thank my wife, Nikita Gupta, for being the difficult-to-please reader, and for having great patience for the cantankerous husband that I sometimes became as I grappled with these stories. To my mother and my brother, I always feel your encouragement with me.

I thank Manasi Subramaniam, my last editor, who believed in this book at the concept stage. I thank Prema Govindan, my current editor at HarperCollins India, who midwifed it. I thank everyone else at my publishers' who helped the book acquire the form that you readers see it in.

Some of the stories here were first published – in different forms and with different names – in various magazines and journals in India. 'Diwali in Muzaffarnagar' was first published as 'Muzaffarnagar Diwali' in the March 2015 issue of *The Caravan*. I thank Chandrahas Choudhury, the magazine's fiction editor at that time, for it. 'The Sad Unknowability of Dilip Singh' and 'Reasonable Limits' were runners-up in consecutive years in the *DNA–Out of Print* Short Fiction contest. I thank Indira Chandrasekhar of *Out of Print* magazine for giving those stories their first light of recognition. 'The Sad Unknowability of Dilip Singh' was published in *DNA* on 27 July 2014; 'Reasonable Limits' was published in the same paper on 22 November 2015. 'B's First

Solo Trip' was first published as 'Diu Is a Dead End' in a now-lapsed online magazine, *The Affair*. 'The Mechanics of Silence' was first published in the Monsoon 2015 issue of *Vayavya*, an online poetry magazine. I thank Vayavya's editor Mihir Vatsa for seeing poetry in that short story.